Judgment Call

Shards of Sevia, Volume 5

E.B. Roshan

Published by Roshan Publishing, 2022.

JUDGMENT CALL

First edition. September 23, 2022.

ISBN: 979-8215706978

Written by E.B. Roshan.

The Characters

Preen Enda: Kiva's fiancee and Rama's widow

Kiva Manjali: Preen's fiance, second cousin and wealthy landowner

Rama Enda: Preen's deceased husband, former bull-rider and Rayad member

Sitabi Enda: Preen and Rama's three-year-old daughter

Arjun Rastikar: Preen's older brother and guardian

Sufya Rastikar: Arjun's Sevian wife

Lashmi Rastikar: Preen's mother (Arjun and Sufya's baby daughter is also named Lashmi, after her grandmother)

Dr. Peter Neyrev: Sevian doctor of anthropology and friend of Preen's deceased father, Amin Rastikar

Oksana Neyrev: Dr. Neyrev's wife

Erkan Durband: traditional tattoo artist and refugee, friend of Preen and Rama

Desh Durband: Erkan's deceased brother, Rayad member

Sanjit Sind: Preen and Rama's old enemy, Rayad member

Manish and Rani Sind: Sanjit's elderly uncle and aunt

Padmi Farhanji: Rais of Dor (province and city) and refugee

Semyon Deshi: Rayad sniper and Rais Padmi's bodyguard

Author's Note:

In the early 1700's, nomadic Tur tribes from Western Asia conquered the land and people of the region now known as Sevia. They ruled it for over two centuries, until the Sevians, a Slavic people native to the region, rebelled against them in 1920, and again in 1953.

After a decade of bloody fighting, the Sevians recaptured the majority of the country, including the capital city of Dor, and drove most of the remaining Tur into the northeastern mountains.

Today, the nation of Sevia is divided into three provinces, symbolized by the three red stars on the national flag. The largest province is Dor. The two smaller provinces, Tur Kej and Tur Fen, function as semi-autonomous states under the rule of Tur Raises (leaders) who are elected for life from the Tur royal family of Farhanji.

Chapter One: Preen

In Sevia's Tur Kej mountains, winter freezes out fall by the end of October most years. Soon I'd be doing the wash in the kitchen instead of the yard. But that day was perfect. It smelled like lemon soap, like dirty things coming clean. It smelled like the color of the beech tree at the end of the yard—such a bright yellow it made me squint.

I swirled clothes around in a big plastic tub and thought about how fast the year was going. Too fast. The New Year and my wedding just around the corner—and I wasn't ready.

My little girl, Sitabi, played by the tubs, popping soap bubbles.

"Kiva's my daddy," she sang, splashing in the water.

That made me jump and drop a dripping towel in the dirt. "What did you say?"

Sitabi flinched. I'd scared her, moving so quick.

Wait, I told myself. Breathe.

She made a face as I brushed the hair out of her eyes with wet fingers.

"What did you say about Kiva?"

"Kiva's my daddy. My very own daddy." She stuck her finger in her mouth.

"He's not."

Rama, her real daddy, bled out on a dirty sidewalk in a city far from our Tur Kej farm. He died in a place she'd seen but didn't remember.

"Why not?" Sitabi stared at me with Rama's dark eyes. Funny how she favored him. No hazel eyes or round cheeks or freckles. Not even one little thing like me. A breeze lifted her hair—she even got those curls from him.

"Did Grandma tell you Kiva was your daddy?"

"No." She looked away. "Kiva told me."

A hot, salty taste rose in my throat. "Kiva told you he was your real daddy?"

Sitabi hunched her shoulders and nodded.

Had Kiva really said that? I punched both fists into the floating clothes. Water splashed onto my sweatpants and made me shiver. "Well, if he did, he's wrong. That isn't true. We've talked about this before. Don't you remember?"

"No." Sitabi slid two more fingers into her mouth.

"Kiva's not your real daddy. But he's going to be your adopted daddy when we get married."

"After the New Year?" Her tense little body relaxed.

"That's right. When we light candles and bake the poppy-seed cakes." I wrung out an undershirt and tossed it into the rinsing tub.

"After the New Year he'll be my real daddy," Sitabi said.

"No."

"No?"

"Kiva loves you very much, but he's not your real daddy. He's not the man who...made you." I bit my tongue. She didn't have to know everything, not yet.

"Oh," said Sitabi. She took her fingers out of her mouth and lifted the sleeve of one of her uncle Arjun's plaid work shirts out of the washtub. I pushed it back, planning what to say.

"A man made me?" Sitabi asked.

"No."

How to explain? Maybe Sitabi needed to hear the story as much as I needed to tell it. "God made you. He makes all babies and gives them to mamas and daddies. But He didn't give you to me and Kiva. He gave you to me and Rama."

"Who's Rama?"

The man who abandoned her and tried to kill me. My first love. "Rama was your real daddy. You have his curly hair."

I reached for her again but Sitabi ducked away.

"Stop it!" she squealed. "Your hands are all wet."

I fished another shirt from the washtub and wrung it out. The skin on my hands felt like shriveled fruit.

"Did you marry Rama at the New Year?" Sitabi asked.

I waited, thinking of what Mother had told me. 'You have to move on, or that precious little one will pay for your mistakes, too.'

"Did you?" Sitabi bounced on her bare toes.

"People don't always get married close to New Year's Day. We got married in the summer. Summer after you were born."

Rama and I met the day he won the bull-riding contest at the autumn fair in Duna. He'd hung onto his bull for longer than I thought anybody could. When he finally hit the ground, I'd been holding my breath so long I saw stars.

With part of his prize money, he bought me heart-shaped pink balloons, the shiny foil kind. We walked around the fairgrounds together and played some of the games.

I'd never tried to put all the bits and pieces of our story together. Not so they'd make sense, anyway. Maybe if I told myself the whole thing from beginning to end, I'd understand how things had gone so quick from pink balloons at the fair to that sweaty afternoon in the hayloft.

My mother was right. Rama's daughter should know who he had been. But not yet.

I didn't know if Sitabi was still listening, but I kept talking. "I was in love. I was scared—and lonely. When you get grown, you better have more sense than I did."

Rama and I shared our first kiss behind a clump of juniper trees between the farmhouse and the cattle barn. After that, the thought of marrying anyone but him was like soda with no fizz.

Rama told me I was his only one forever.

I told him I'd been promised to Kiva Manjali since we were children.

Kiva's family already owned most of the land we Rastikars pastured our herds on. He was tall and handsome. Kind. Generous. Good without trying too hard. The perfect husband—except he wasn't Rama.

I focused on the bubbles in the wash water, so I wouldn't have to look at Sitabi. She was too young to know that the wedding should come before the baby. Would she be ashamed of Rama and me someday?

A few weeks before my father died, one of our rich neighbors offered him ten cows for me. Father was half out of his head with pain and too weak to refuse.

My older brother, Arjun, took one look at the fat, greedy face of that neighbor fellow and told him to forget it.

The man didn't seem to understand what 'No' meant. He kept coming back, pestering Arjun and Mother both. His eyes followed me everywhere. Them, and his hands. Once I dreamed him with spiders for hands.

That's when Rama made his plan. Rama said if he got me pregnant, my family would let us marry without a bride price. He would never have been able to afford the one my family needed, so it seemed the only way.

The barn was usually empty on those long summer days, so we climbed into the hayloft. We scrambled over piles of dusty bales to the very back.

Rama tried to be gentle. It hurt some, but that wasn't why I cried. When I tried to explain, Rama didn't understand. He got mad at himself for hurting me and left me lying there in the hay.

"Mama?" Sitabi's squeaky voice brought me back to the washtubs. "Where's Rama? Where's my real daddy?"

"He died."

"Rama died?"

"Yes."

"A long time ago?"

"Not so long."

Sitabi was quiet. Those dark eyes didn't show me what she was thinking.

"You were little the last time you saw your real daddy—probably too little to remember. But he loved you very much. He named you Sitabi, like the princess in the story, because you were his princess."

A flash of color down by our barn caught my eye. Kiva walked out into the sunshine, brushing dust from his red plaid shirt. I'd hoped he'd stay busy helping Arjun until I had the wash hung out because I didn't want to talk with him right then.

Sitabi took a second longer to notice him. When she did, her face lit up. She spread her arms and sprinted toward him down the dirt path.

"Kiva! I want a ride," she yelled. "Give me a shoulder ride!"

"No, not now." Kiva said, laughing. "I'll make you stink and your Mama will be mad." Those two loved each other like they shared blood. What was wrong with me that I didn't smile to see that tall, handsome redhead with my little snip of a girl? Why couldn't I be happy that I had another chance at love and a good life? Everybody else was.

I leaned close over the washtub, swirling the clothes around like I was doing something important. A blue dress of Sitabi's rose to the surface. Rama had bought it for her when we lived in Dor. It was too small now, but I still let her wear it.

"Preen!" Kiva called, waving to me across the yard. "Need some help?"

As he came close, the smell of sweat and muck wafted off him—sour, but not a bad sour. He was breathing hard from loading the cattle trailer, and strands of matted hair hung in his face.

"You finished quick." I pushed the clothes up and down in the cloudy water.

"We're only bringing Brown and those three yearlings to the fair this year. Didn't Arjun tell you?"

"No." I focused on the patched, rolled-up sleeves and the sweat stains at his armpits. Easier than looking into his face. If our eyes met, he'd know right away I wasn't happy with him. If I wanted him to understand why, I'd have to explain. When I was alone with my little girl, finding the right words came easy, but add another person and my tongue tripped itself up.

"So loading wasn't a problem," Kiva said. "Even though Brown likes to put up a fight." He laughed and stretched. The muscles in his arms bulged under black tattoos. "Gets meaner every day. I'm going to be sore tomorrow. And—" He turned to show me a big smear of manure down the back of his jeans. "Sorry. More work for you."

"You slipped?"

"Twice." He laughed again.

Sitabi laughed, too.

"Nothing like a little tussle with a bull to make me thankful I don't make my money riding," he said.

I dropped Sitabi's blue dress into the rinse tub and wiped my wrinkly hands on my sweatpants.

"You've got to give me credit for some sense. Didn't want my brains shaken into porridge."

I frowned so he'd know he'd said the wrong thing.

"I actually did want to be a bull-rider when I was a kid," he added quickly. "Crazy bull threw me five meters the first time. I didn't have the guts to get back on." Kiva stopped, maybe sensing that not all the coldness came from the breeze. His smile disappeared. "Preen, what's wrong?"

I made myself look into his face. "Why did you tell Sitabi you're her father?"

Those green eyes of his clouded. "Well, obviously I didn't mean—"

"Why would you say that?"

"As far as she's concerned, I am her real father. The man who put her inside you didn't deserve the name."

"I could understand that coming from her grandmother, but you?" I tried to cough the scratchiness out of my throat. "The little thing's so confused."

"She wouldn't be confused if you didn't keep bringing up Rama."

Sitabi began dropping bits of hay into the wash water.

"Stop it," I snapped.

She didn't.

I smacked her.

Our eyes filled with tears at the same time. She ran into the house, bawling, but I stayed where I was.

"Why does everyone want to pretend that Rama never existed?" I bit my lip so hard it started to bleed. That hurt less than trying to hold in my sadness. "We were married more than two years. He was her father."

Kiva reached for me. "I just want everything to be all right again. To be like it was before."

I shrugged his hand off. "Before? What does that even mean?"

"You're mine," Kiva said. "You've always been. There's nothing you can do that would make me love you any less."

That was true. If there was, I'd already done it.

"And Sitabi makes the deal sweeter." He smiled.

He could melt me with that smile if I let him. Only— "You'd take a sponge and wipe the last three years clean away if you could."

"You're right. I would." The green in his eyes went steely-gray.

"If you did, there'd be no Sitabi," I said. "Don't you understand? No Rama—no Sitabi. No Rama—no me." My parents had picked Kiva for me. I'd picked Rama for myself.

"Why, Preen?"

"I loved him." My voice sounded like gravel. I loved Kiva too, even though it wasn't the same. Couldn't ever be the same, not after how me and Rama had ended. Someday he'd understand. Maybe.

He grabbed my hand and squeezed my chapped knuckles so hard it hurt. "I loved you first. Long before that piece of—"

I set my teeth. "So it's like when kids fight over a toy? 'I saw it first!' 'No, I touched it first!'"

He let go. The pink sunburn on his nose and cheekbones turned red. I ducked back to the washtub before he got the idea to reach for me again.

"You better go clean up before we eat, if you're staying. I need to get the wash on the line."

He didn't leave.

I didn't want him there, but I also didn't want to be alone with nothing but the slosh and slap of the clothes. So I was glad he didn't leave.

"I'm going to buy you a big automatic washing machine," Kiva said. "It will fit just right in our new kitchen."

"Mmmm."

"I heard the appliance place got a shipment last week. They should still have some good ones. I'll get a dryer, too, if I can."

"We've got the sun. Don't need a dryer."

"But what if I want you to have one?"

Chapter Two: Preen

The day of the Autumn Fair in Duna, we all got an early start. The light coming through the window still looked grey when the alarm on my phone beeped.

Outside, someone cranked the generator and it began its all-day rumble. A second later, the tea kettle whistled from the kitchen.

I got up and washed my face. Since I'd shaved my head for Rama only a few months before, I could still smooth my hair down with wet fingers.

Sitabi's little bare feet stuck off the edge of the mattress we shared on the guest room floor. I shook her, but she kept snoring.

That gave me another minute, so I dug around in my jewelry box, looking for earrings. My fingers brushed a velvet bag at the bottom. I didn't have to open it to know what was inside. Kiva's fifteenth birthday present to me—a silver nose ring set with jade that had once belonged to his grandmother.

Since coming home from Dor, I hardly wore traditional jewelry anymore. I lifted it, balancing the weight on my palm for a moment before slipping it into my nose. Seeing his gift on me would make him smile.

If Kiva wanted to go back to those easy days, before Rama and Dor, maybe the best thing for Sitabi and me was to go along with him. He was certain he could be so good and kind that I'd just have to forget I'd ever loved anybody but him. Maybe he was right—but he didn't know the whole story.

When I finally got Sitabi to rouse, she squeezed her eyes shut and started to whimper. I gave her a little shake. "Crying girls don't go to the fair."

That silenced her. She wiped her nose on the blanket and hopped out of bed. After I washed her, I fastened bells around her ankles, so if she got away from me at the fair, I could track her by the noise. She ran like a rabbit about every time I turned my back.

When we were both dressed, we joined the others in the kitchen.

My brother, Arjun, stirred a pot of porridge on the stove while his pretty blonde wife, Sufya, tried to soothe their baby girl. Lashmi was too young for 'No fair day for you' threats.

Kiva came in from the barn and sat down at the kitchen table.

I poured him a cup of tea with hot milk.

"I didn't think you'd kept that nose ring," he said softly. "I thought you'd lost it, or sold it in Dor, or something."

"I'd never do that." I'd never lose a family heirloom. Only the family honor.

He reached across the kitchen table and stroked my cheek with one finger. "You look so pretty today."

I backed away. The memory of Rama's warm hands made my stomach clench so hard it hurt. We'd loved each other, Rama and I. Love as strong as death—almost. If Kiva knew everything I knew, would he ever touch me again?

My Sitabi came over, jingling at every step. She snuggled against him like his side was her place and stuffed bread into her mouth.

He stroked her head and twisted her short braids around his fingers. "What are you and Mama going to do today, Baby Girl?"

"We're coming with you to the fair!" she shouted, puffing out crumbs.

"Oh? You must be excited."

Sitabi's smile came fast and rare, like her daddy's. "Mama said if I didn't cry, she'd take me."

Kiva glanced up at me, eyebrows raised.

I nodded.

"I didn't think you were coming this year," he said. "Your mother told me—"

"Sitabi talked me into it." I probably shouldn't have promised I'd take her, but that little girl could be persuasive.

He was quiet for a minute. "I thought it might be—" He cut himself off.

I waited.

He sipped his tea.

"Might be what?" I asked.

"Too soon." If it was too soon for us to be seen together in town, why wasn't it too soon for us to be preparing for our wedding?

"It might be hard for you, seeing people we know," he said.

I shrugged. Would we spend the rest of our lives together thinking things we couldn't tell each other?

"With all the refugees coming in, I might see somebody I knew in Dor," I added, just to say something.

Arjun thumped the porridge pot down on the table and began ladling the gray, gloppy stuff into bowls. "Eat quick," he said. "Big Brown is ready for action."

"I'm glad you're coming to the fair," Kiva said after a minute.

I stopped eating and looked up. "Really?"

He wasn't stupid—he knew people traded pitying looks behind his back. But he didn't seem to care. At least not as much as I would. I'd rather have people hate me than feel sorry for me.

"Of course." Kiva smiled.

Oh, he was good-looking when he smiled. Strong jaw and cheekbones. Eyes the color of old moss on a stone. Girls had been throwing themselves at him as long as I could remember, but he'd been like the fox in the story, crazy for the one he couldn't get.

***

Outside, I held Sitabi up so she could peek at Brown, Arjun's big bull, through one of the tiny windows in the livestock trailer. It creaked as the cattle inside bumped against each other, stirring up whiffs of manure and warm hide. Other than a few white flecks on his chest, Brown was red-brown all over, almost the same shade as Kiva's hair.

Kiva and Arjun had wound strips of cloth around the blunted tips of his horns, like they always did with the contest bulls. Not that the cloth would help a rider much if he found himself hooked on one.

With a grunt, Brown turned to look at the three of us. His small, sleepy eyes glinted.

"Say goodbye," I told Sitabi. "Brown will be going home with someone else today."

"Bye." She waved.

Brown had been our herd's stud while Arjun saved for a bigger, better one.

This year was finally going to be the year. Kiva had agreed to buy Arjun a bull as part of my bride price—the best he could afford. They'd share it between them, alternating breeding seasons.

"Nothing's too good for our first year together," Kiva said. His eyes softened with pride as he scanned the hillside pasture above us. The cattle grazed slow and steady, all facing the same way. Kiva put his arm around my shoulders. "Next spring we'll be seeing the best calves yet."

I found myself leaning into him, letting Sitabi's weight settle between us.

***

Once we'd crammed ourselves into Kiva's truck, he revved the engine and away we went.

"You betting anything on Big Brown?" Kiva asked, leaning over to poke Arjun in the ribs.

Arjun pushed him away. "He's seen better days. Safer to bet on the rider this year."

"You think I'd let you bring a bull I wouldn't bet on?" Kiva said.

They laughed together. Every year, Kiva and Arjun argued about which bull we'd bring for the bull-riding competition, and Kiva usually got his way. It was almost a family tradition.

Our truck hit a rut in the dirt road and we all bounced. Behind us, in the trailer, the cattle bumped around and grunted.

I shifted Sitabi onto my knees for a little more breathing room. Mother pressed against me on one side and Sufya on the other. The sharp edge of the picnic basket they'd packed earlier that morning put pins and needles in my leg.

All the way down to Duna everyone talked loud and cheerful about nothing, like they were afraid if they didn't keep their mouths working someone would let the big question slip—Preen, aren't you ashamed to be seen in town?

Fair day crowded out the streets in Duna, like always. Cars and trucks from miles around, even as far as the Tur Fen border, parked in rows in the vacant lot just outside town where the fair was held. The beech trees between the livestock pens dropped yellow leaves across the dirt paths. The sky looked even bluer between those shaking, shining leaves.

We parked as close to the picnic pavilions as we could. Mother took the picnic basket. Sufya hoisted baby Lashmi higher on her hip and followed.

Sufya's face looked how I felt when I first arrived in Dor—curious and eager, but also a little dazed because of too many new things happening at once.

"We'll find us a good spot," Mother called back to Arjun and Kiva. "Come after the bull-riding contest, or whenever you get hungry."

I didn't follow her and Sufya, and nobody asked why not.

Kiva led the three yearlings out of the trailer, using a long metal rod with a hook on it that went through the rings in their noses. Sitabi and I watched.

When I lived in Dor, a Sevian friend once asked me if I found it ironic that in the Tur provinces, both women and cattle wore rings in their noses. I didn't have a good answer for that.

When only Brown was left in the trailer, Kiva jumped back into the cab and drove off toward the bull-riding ring.

"Want to go look around, Baby Girl?" I asked Sitabi.

She nodded.

Everything about the fair was the same as the last time I'd gone—except not. Behind the restless cattle in the livestock pens stood a long row of booths. The old women there were selling things my grandmother would have used, only because she had to. Who actually wanted hand-embroidered vests and traditional skirts anymore? Or serving bowls made of glazed pottery?

People wanted trendy jeans and blouses made in Dor. They'd rather buy plastic mixing bowls that wouldn't break if you dropped them.

Sitabi squeezed the beaded fringes on my skirt and watched everything with eyes like a baby owl.

I'd loved the fair too when I was younger. Now it felt small and sad and desperate, like our Tur people were clinging to what remained of the past because it was all we had left. The haze of wood smoke and dust over the grounds made everything look unreal, like the wind could blow it away.

Memories drew me toward the bull-riding ring at the center of the fairground. I swung Sitabi onto my hip. "Let's go see where your daddy used to ride."

"My real daddy?"

"Yes. Rama."

When I was a little younger, I used to stand near the fence to watch the riders, enjoying the guilty thrill of their eyes following me.

Then Rama came down from Tur Fen, like the hero in the song about the Moon Girl, and the others faded away. He rode his bull, ate dirt, collected his prize money and came to find me—the one quiet girl in a cheering crowd.

Rama was eighteen then, three years older than me, but he already walked stiff sometimes. The first two fingers on his right hand bent sideways. His right shoulder hurt so bad he carried a bottle of pain pills in his jacket pocket.

Now I was eighteen, and I'd already done all the big things my life could hold. At least that's how I felt. Sometimes I wondered what on earth God was thinking to let me still be alive.

Rama used to talk about how we'd have a nice apartment in Dor someday. Leather sofa. Big windows. A sports car. Anything we wanted.

I didn't care much about all that, but when he told me I made him a better person, happiness swelled my heart so big it hurt. I was sure God had chosen me to make Rama the man he should be—to save him. Instead, I killed him.

Chapter Three: Preen

I saw Erkan Durband before he saw me. He was standing right up against the bull-ring fence with his hands on the top rail, looking down into the empty ring. Even if he hadn't been wearing his yellow sport jacket with 'DENISOVICH' on the back, I would have known who it was, because he'd somehow brought Dor into the mountains with him. Memories of war hung around him like smoke. I could almost hear the gunfire. My heart began to pound.

Sitabi squirmed. "Down, Mommy. Put me down."

I let her slide to the ground. "Erkan?"

He turned. For a minute we stared at each other, not sure what to say. Then his scarred face melted into happy surprise. "Preen! I never thought I'd see you again. Even here..."

"We live up the road," I said. "It's not far."

"I never thought I'd see you again," he repeated softly, shaking his head.

"We come to Duna all the time. But how did you get here?"

"Long story," he said. "The short version is, Dr. Neyrev sent me. You know he and his wife were in prison, right?" Erkan never could talk about himself more than two seconds.

"I heard. Are you helping the refugees, too?"

He glanced down at his expensive shoes, splattered with mud and dung. "I am one."

"Oh." I should have guessed.

"They let Mrs. Neyrev go pretty quickly, but they held Dr. Neyrev at Riverside Prison for months without even a trial," Erkan said. "He got pneumonia and almost died. That's the only reason they released him. Scared he'd die on their hands."

"I didn't know that." Shame on me. It must have been only a few weeks after his release that Dr. Neyrev came to visit us. Why they had allowed him to travel to a Tur province, I had no idea. He'd looked terrible—pale, gray, wrinkled—but I didn't care. I barely noticed, let alone bothered to ask how he was doing. Saving Rama had been the only important thing in the world then.

Kiva's laugh rang out behind us.

Sitabi popped her head out from around my skirt to see him.

A little voice inside me warned, 'Better if Kiva and Erkan never meet,' but it was already too late.

"Who's this, Preen?" Kiva asked. In a second, his face went from startled to horrified to wary. Erkan's looks could take some getting used to.

"I'm a friend from Dor." Erkan paused, like he was waiting for Kiva to say something. "Friend of Rama's. We lived in the same apartment block. Actually Rama was my younger brother's best friend."

"Kiva's my fiance," I said.

Erkan nodded.

"It's nice to meet you," Kiva said. He reached over and wrapped his hand around my arm, like he thought he might need to protect me.

"Erkan's the one who rescued me from Sanjit." The words came out jerky because of how hard my heart was beating. "I wouldn't be here today if it wasn't for him. I might not even be alive."

Erkan wasn't the only one to rescue me. Kiva and Arjun had done their part, too. But I didn't like the way Kiva was looking at Erkan.

Kiva's fingers tightened on my arm. "I'm sorry," he said after a long pause. "She's told me about you, of course. But I didn't realize—"

Erkan shrugged. "Of course. How could you know who I was?"

"Right." Kiva gave him a stiff smile. He didn't seem to know where to look. "I had no idea. She never mentioned—"

"The scar tissue that used to be my face? No worries, it's not something people usually notice." He laughed. "I was going to watch the bull-riding contest. Never seen one, except on TV. Can you believe it?" He rubbed the un-scarred side of his face.

Kiva stuffed his hands into his jacket pockets. He looked like he'd rather be in the shed, getting ready to ride a bull, then out talking with us.

The place where his hand had been on my arm turned cold in the breeze.

"If there's ever anything we can do for you..." Kiva cleared his throat. "I know it wasn't easy getting her out of Sanjit's hands. You risked a lot. You said before you wouldn't take money, but—"

Don't say it, Kiva, I shouted inside my head. Don't offer him money.

Erkan turned and rested his elbows on the splintery fence. "Loan me five dinars? I was going to bet on the contest but I forgot my wallet at the hotel."

"Why not?" Kiva fished a ragged twenty-dinar note out of his back pocket. "Please. Any time."

All of a sudden, I was so mad I wanted to smack him. Did he think Erkan needed payment for rescuing me?

Silence as thick as the pale dust settled around us. Erkan looked from Kiva to me. Even with only one good eye, he couldn't miss the the shame heating up my face. How could Kiva be so stupid as to think he was being kind?

"Good luck," Kiva said. "Don't bet on the big brown bull with white flecks on his chest."

One corner of Erkan's mouth turned up. "I won't." He folded the twenty dinar note exactly in half, creased it, and slipped it into his pocket.

The sounds of the fair—people shouting, cattle bellowing, music blaring—filled my ears again. How come Kiva always knew what to say? He made fixing mistakes look easy. But I was still mad at him.

Chapter Four: Kiva

Arjun and I unloaded Brown into his holding pen by the bull-riding ring. He ran down the narrow chute to the far end and banged his horns on the gate. He kept pushing against the bars and snorting, like the noise spooked him.

I leaned over and slapped his dusty rear. "Good luck, Brown!"

"It's after ten," Arjun held up his phone. "Time to pick up that monster you're paying too much for."

I laughed. "He's worth every dinar. And so is she."

I was climbing into the truck when I caught sight of Preen on the other side of the bull-riding ring. A fellow in a yellow jacket stood beside her.

Sitabi skittered around the two of them, tugging on Preen's skirt. Preen didn't pay her any mind, so whatever that fellow was saying must have been important. Or he was important—whoever he was.

Preen's fine. Just go, I told myself. But I couldn't. I jumped out of my truck and started toward them. So what if Preen thought I didn't trust her? Maybe I didn't.

She jumped when I came up behind them, and started talking, fast and nervous. "This is Erkan," she said. "He's the one who saved me from Sanjit." She looked at me like she expected me to kiss his feet or something.

Before I could answer, my phone buzzed. Most likely it was the trader asking if I was on my way. He'd told me to be at the sale pens by ten-thirty. I left my phone in my pocket and we stood there, staring at each other. Me, Preen, Sitabi, and this Erkan. The refugee from Dor. The hero.

I tried not to stare—never saw anybody burned like him. Half his face shriveled, blotchy red. One eye gone. Maybe in Dor people wouldn't think he was anything unusual, even with that face, but in the

Tur Kej hills, he showed up like a fresh brand. The trendy jeans, short hair, and cocky swagger spelled OUTSIDER.

What am I doing? I thought. I don't have time for this.

But I couldn't pull myself away, not with him looking at Preen like that. Not with them looking at each other like that.

Even if they were just friends, it was already too much. They talked like I wasn't standing right there. God help me, but I was glad Erkan's face was so badly scarred, because he must have been a good-looking fellow before it happened.

My breakfast turned sour in my stomach. Why on earth should I be jealous of a refugee with half his face burned? No good reason, except Erkan was Preen's neighbor and her friend during the two biggest years of her life. The two years that changed her from a girl to a woman. The two years she spent without me.

I'd been in love with Preen as long as I could remember. Come the New Year, she'd be my wife. But would we ever be friends?

Never in my life had I wanted something so bad I ached for it, and never had I been less certain I'd get it. The smiles and presents and as pretty a house as any woman could want hadn't brought me nearer to Preen than I'd been three years ago, back when I still thought she loved me. Preen had agreed to marry me—for honor, for the family—that was settled. But I wanted her heart.

From the day I was born to the day Preen said 'No' to me and 'Yes' to Rama, life had pretty much gone my way. No denying it, I'd been spoiled. My mother and two older sisters made sure of that.

Nobody but Preen ever stood up to me. She was seven years younger, but that didn't stop her. That's why I fell for her. She told it to me like it was.

Preen's mother, Lashmi, was my mother's cousin, so we saw a lot of each other growing up, even before the families decided she and I were a perfect match.

When Preen's father died, I moved up from Duna to help Arjun on his family's farm. That was a hundred times better than stocking shelves in Manjali Fashions and Fabrics, my family's store. It seemed natural that Preen's life and mine would flow together. Until Preen told me she was carrying Rama's baby, I was sure she felt the same way. The truth was like going to sleep in the hayloft and waking up in the manure pile.

"Never thought I'd see you again." Erkan kept staring at her, shaking his head.

"Is Dunya here, too?" Preen asked him.

Sitabi started tugging on her again. Preen picked her up.

Whoever Dunya was, she must have been somebody Erkan didn't like. His shoulders stiffened at the sound of her name. "No."

"Is she...she's all right?" Preen asked. "She got out of Camp Peace?"

"Oh, yes. She got out." Erkan pushed the words past his teeth like they tasted bad.

The worried wrinkles smoothed from Preen's forehead. "I'm so glad."

"Mama! Come see more cows!" Sitabi yelled.

"In a minute. Now, hush."

"As far as I know, Dunya's fine." Erkan said. "I haven't spoken with her in a while."

"She went to Germany?"

"No. She's in Dovni. Married a fat Sevian guy with a fishing business down there, or something." Erkan stuck his hands in his pockets and looked out over the fairgrounds like he had no plans to go anywhere for a long time.

I thought about what I could say to make him move on without being downright rude. He had rescued Preen, after all.

"Kiva, Kiva, I want to see the new bull!" Sitabi grabbed my shirt in both hands and started bouncing up and down in her mama's arms.

"Later, Baby Girl. I've got to go get him first—already late."

"We'll see you back at the pavilions for lunch," Preen said, not looking at me.

Was she planning to introduce Erkan to the rest of her family?

Erkan gave me a stiff nod. I took off toward the truck, jogging. I'd already paid a hefty deposit on that stud, and the trader said if I was too late, the deal was off.

When I looked back, Preen and Erkan were still standing together, still talking about people from Dor I'd never met and places in Dor I'd never seen.

Something Erkan said made Preen smile.

Erkan better not have cost us our stud bull, I thought. And he better stay away from Preen after today. She's mine. I'm not going to lose her again.

Chapter Five: Preen

Sitabi squirmed in my arms. "Down! Down!" she shouted. "I want to go with Kiva!" "Hush," I said. "Kiva's busy. We'll go find him when it's time to eat."

Sitabi always picked Kiva over me. No surprise. Kiva didn't have to do anything to make everyone love him except be Kiva.

Rama, now, love didn't come easy to him. Would his little daughter have changed that, if he'd made it back to her?

Erkan pulled a box of cigarettes from his back pocket and lit one. "So that's your fiance." He offered the box to me. I waved it away, but he didn't seem to notice and kept holding it out.

"I don't smoke, remember?"

"Oh. Right." He glanced after Kiva, whose height and red hair made him easy to spot in the crowd. "He seems like a good guy."

"He is."

"In his own way."

"He wasn't trying to shame you," I said. "It's just—meeting someone Rama used to know in Dor—he doesn't like it."

Erkan shrugged. "If a guy ran off with my girlfriend, and lived someplace, I wouldn't like that guy either. Or that place. Or his friends." He chewed the end of his cigarette. "Or his dog."

The crowd around the bull-ring had been growing while we talked. They started hooting and yelling so loud we moved close to hear each other better.

Erkan's shoulder brushed against mine. His smoke drifted around us both. The bitter smell brought back all those nights I waited up for Rama in our little apartment in Dor.

On the far side of the bull-ring, two men opened one of the sliding gates.

A shiny black bull with red ribbons tied to his horns came leaping and twisting across the packed ground. It threw itself into the air, all four hoofs off the ground at once.

The crowd screamed. Some of the boys perched on top of the fence took off their jackets and waved them. The rider's legs flew up. He caught himself, rolled, and collapsed on the ground in a puff of dust.

The bull plunged around the ring until the men at the gates herded him out.

Erkan lit himself another cigarette. "I'm not surprised Rama was a bull-rider. He had guts."

The old bitter taste rose in my throat. "Tell that to my family."

"Let's go," Sitabi whined. Her head drooped heavy on my shoulder and drool left a wet spot on my sleeve.

"I may be biased, seeing as I owe him my life." Erkan blew smoke out through his teeth. "But I'm entitled to my opinion. He was brave. Brave as they come."

I closed my eyes to shut out Erkan's face and saw Rama's, streaked with grit and tears, moments before he died. How many times would I have to relive killing him?

"Does Kiva know Sanjit kidnapped you to get back at Rama?" Erkan asked.

"No."

"Might be worth explaining. Does he know how Rama died?"

I bit the inside of my lip. "Why do you care?"

Erkan gave me a long look out of his good eye. "What does he know?"

"About me and Rama?"

"Sure."

"Or what happened when I went back to Dor to find him?"

"Yes, everything. How much of the story does he know?"

I took a long breath. "Well—"

Another gate rattled open and Brown, Arjun's bull, charged out, twisting like a fish on the end of a line. "Kiva would rather pretend my life with Rama never happened."

Erkan laughed. "I like to pretend lots of things never happened, but every time I look in the mirror, I have to start convincing myself all over again."

"I'm hungry, Mama," Sitabi yawned, showing her little white teeth.

"You should come back to the pavilions with us," I told Erkan. "Have some tea, at least."

He picked at a splinter on the fence with his tattooed fingers. "The contest isn't over."

I shrugged. "Come back later, then. They'll be riding all morning."

He was quiet again for a minute. "My brother would have loved this. Desh." He jerked his chin toward the action in the bull-ring. "In a different life, he'd have been a bull-rider."

Brown's rider lay flat on his back on the ground. It was hard to tell if he was knocked out, or just winded.

"Personally, I struggle to see the appeal. Sprains. Bruises. Permanent brain damage." Erkan laughed again, a dry laugh, more like a cough.

"Not as dangerous as fighting for Rayad," I said.

"I didn't have much choice about that. One night I went to sleep a tattoo artist, and woke up a Rayad fighter, with White Horses screaming in my face."

"I thought you'd joined Rayad when Desh did."

"Guilt by association." Erkan shrugged. "You know, there's one other thing I've never understood. I wasn't Rama's friend. Desh was. But it was me he saved."

His sunken shoulders and clenched hands showed how hard the memories came. "Some White Horses took the three of us—me, Rama, Desh—out into the street behind the building where they'd been holding us. Big gray factory building near the river. They told Desh they didn't need him anymore; he was free to go. They told him to run home."

Erkan tapped the fence rail lightly with his fist. "When Desh was little, he used to have nightmares about wolves chasing him. Wolves and wildcats. He'd climb into my bed and push his sweaty head right under my chin and go back to sleep and snore."

I held my breath. Erkan's flat voice turned me inside out.

"Desh didn't move. He wasn't going to run for them, so they shot him right there in front of us. Then they grabbed me." Erkan twisted up his face like he was watching his brother's murder over again.

You don't have to talk about it, I wanted to tell him, but the words didn't come.

"I offered my soul to God, but He must not have wanted it."

"Then Rama...?"

"Yes. About five seconds before I went to be with Desh, Rama started yelling at Maxim Porofky. 'Don't do it! I know what you want to know. We can work something out.'"

A lump rose in my throat.

"The minute he said that, he was dead, and he knew it," Erkan said. "Even if he escaped from the White Horses, our Rais would have him killed for spilling Rayad secrets. But I'd have a chance." Erkan shook his head slowly. "Rama watched his best friend murdered and didn't lift a finger to stop it. But for some reason, for me..."

I swallowed a whole mouthful of tears.

Erkan looked straight at me. "Wish I could have asked Rama, 'Why me? Why not Desh?'"

We were both quiet. Around us, people hooted and yelled as another bull spun circles in the dust, but the noise seemed far away.

"I miss him," Erkan said.

"Me too," I whispered, then realized he meant his brother Desh, not Rama.

"Mama?" Sitabi stirred against my side. "Mama?" She poked a finger into my cheek. "Let's go eat with Grandma and Kiva."

Guilt replaced the sadness in my stomach. Kiva wouldn't like it that I was still with Erkan. "I should go. Sitabi's hungry."

Erkan straightened and looked around, like he'd just woken up. "Me too. I've got a client coming to see me at the hotel this afternoon. Needs some old ink touched up."

He tossed the burnt-out stub of his cigarette into the dirt. "It was good to see you again, Preen. Really good. I hope you're...I hope Kiva is..." He touched my arm. "Rama was a lucky guy. Kiva is, too." His hand dropped.

I looked down at my feet, confused and scared by the longing in Erkan's face. How could I have missed it before? No wonder he and Kiva hadn't liked each other much.

"You and Kiva should talk more," he said as Sitabi and I walked away.

Chapter Six: Preen

Sitabi and I wandered back towards the wooden picnic pavilions, where women heated pots on gas burners and buttered bread for sandwiches. Little kids chased each other around, screaming.

Stepping into the shade of the pavilion, I caught a thread of talk.

"...lucky Kiva still wants her," a woman in a black dress with purple flowers was telling my mother.

Mother stood silent, wrapping the ribbons braided into her hair around her fingers. She hadn't shaved her head for Father—he'd asked her not to—but she only wore white ribbons now.

Sufya sat on a blanket beside her sleeping baby. She patted Lashmi's back as she glanced from one woman to the other.

"But if she were my daughter..." the woman sighed and shook her head.

Mother still didn't say anything. Maybe she felt the same way.

The pavilion seemed chilly after a morning spent in the sunshine. I almost walked back out, but they'd already seen me.

"Isn't there a new scandal to talk about by this time?" I asked.

The woman in the black and purple dress turned around. For a moment, she looked ashamed. Then her face settled into a smug half-smile.

I knew her after all—Kiva's aunt on his father's side. That part of his family lived so far away we saw them only once or twice a year.

We shared a scowl. Too bad I hadn't stayed at the bull-ring a few more minutes and given her time to go somewhere else.

Sufya glanced my way with worried eyes. Her Tur still wasn't good enough to follow our conversation, but she must be able to tell we weren't happy.

"Have you made any sandwiches yet?" I asked her in Sev. "Sitabi's hungry and the men will be back soon."

"We were waiting for you to come." Sufya gave her daughter a final pat and got to her feet. Her long blonde ponytail swished across her shoulders. She went to the table and began slicing bread.

The smell of garlic drifted through the air as Mother ripped the paper off a package of sausage links.

Sitabi squirmed from my arms and ran to her. "Sausage, please!" She held out both hands, fingers spread wide.

Mother cut her a slice of sausage. "Wait for the bread," she said, but Sitabi didn't, just like I couldn't when I was little.

"You'd better eat too, Preen."

I crossed my arms over my chest and hugged myself, feeling the ribs through my shirt. These days, I only ate to make Mother stop pestering me about how thin I'd gotten. "Later."

Kiva's aunt stood around a little longer, watching us make sandwiches. Then she huffed and marched out of the pavilion.

Mother's face relaxed as she watched me spread butter on a piece of bread for Sitabi. She didn't say anything. Maybe she thought I hadn't heard what Kiva's aunt said. After all, no point in bringing it up if I hadn't.

What was the aunt's name, anyway? Desi? Seeli? I told myself it didn't matter what an old woman in a flowered dress thought about us. If Kiva didn't care, why should I?

***

Kiva's voice carried well. "It was just ten minutes!" he yelled.

I looked up to see him and Arjun coming toward us across the fairgrounds.

Arjun's face flushed red as people turned around to to see what the fuss was about. He grabbed Kiva's wrist and said something I couldn't hear. Kiva shook him off.

"I'm ten minutes late, and that stinking trader sells my bull!" He flung his arms out.

"The whole world doesn't need to know," Arjun said.

My stomach dropped.

"Oh, no," Mother said softly.

Arjun and Kiva joined us in the pavilion. Sweat and dust streaked the wavy lines tattooed on their arms. Getting the bulls ready for the contest was quite a chore.

Kiva rubbed his hands on his jeans to clean them, stalked over and grabbed a sandwich from the stack Mother had piled on a plate.

Sufya's eyes went wide. "What's wrong?" she asked Arjun in Sev. "What happened?"

He smiled at her. "No big problem. Only a bad..." He hesitated, sorting through Sev words in his mind. "A trade gone bad. We didn't get our bull."

Kiva sat down heavily on the edge of the blanket farthest from Lashmi. His chest rose and fell in a long sigh. "Turns out he's the same one that ripped off Manish Sind a few years back. Would have been nice to know that beforehand."

I filled a cup of milky tea from the thermos and brought it to him. He took it with a nod.

Someone a few pavilions away started up a dance tune on a fiddle, fast but sad. A little hand drum joined in.

"Where's your friend?" Kiva asked through a mouthful of bread and meat.

"You mean Erkan?" He should know I didn't have friends anymore.

"Yes, Erkan."

"I'm not sure. He might have left and gone back to Holiday Home. That's where he's staying." I pictured Erkan wandering through the fairgrounds alone. He was as Tur as any of us, but still a foreigner here in the hills.

"Just as well."

I stiffened. "I told him he should join us for lunch. He didn't want to. Probably because you shamed him, offering him money like he was a beggar."

"Just as well," Kiva muttered again. He brushed crumbs from his beard.

Lots of things I wanted to say came to mind, but nothing slipped out except, "Why?"

Kiva didn't seem to hear me. "I can't believe it," he groaned. "That trader is a snake."

Arjun grunted in agreement and sipped his own tea.

"I'm sorry that happened." I sat down beside Kiva on the blanket and ran a hand through his hair, twisting the knotted strands between my fingers like I used to do with Rama. "You should have gone to meet him sooner. Erkan didn't care about talking with you."

"You're right about that," he said grimly.

Heat rushed into my face. "Just because you're mad about getting cheated over a bull, you don't have to—"

"That's not it, Preen."

I turned away, seething inside. Words never came easy when I wanted them most. "I'm going to take a couple of these sandwiches down to the bull-ring and see if Erkan's still there. He looked starved. No telling when he last ate."

Kiva put his own sandwich down on the blanket. "No, you won't."

I narrowed my eyes at him and made to get up.

His fingers locked around my wrist. "I said no. That fellow is trouble."

My heart beat faster. I remembered Erkan's arms around me as we stood together in the darkness between the rows of tents in Camp Peace, squeezing like he didn't dare let go.

Kiva's voice broke into my thoughts. "You're not going off with Erkan again."

"You're hurting me," I whispered.

He dropped my arm like it was hot. "I'm sorry. Please—"

I scrambled to my feet. "What do you mean, Erkan's trouble? He protected me. Sanjit hated Rama enough to do anything to get even, but Erkan tricked him into letting me go."

"Preen—" Kiva's green eyes turned soft.

"And I didn't 'go off with Erkan.'" I rubbed my wrist, even though it didn't hurt anymore. "You don't trust me. That's what it is. I'm always going to be the girl who ran off and broke your heart."

"That's not—"

"Yes it is. You're scared that if you let me out of your sight, I'll do it again."

Kiva lowered his eyes and started flicking breadcrumbs off the blanket. "Erkan's a wreck."

"It's not his fault his face is like that." I turned to stop Sitabi from dropping her sandwich.

"I'm not talking about his face."

"You don't know nothing about him."

Sitabi dropped her bread face-down, picked it up again and took a big bite. Butter and dirt made a brown ring around her mouth. I snatched the bread away and threw it far enough so she wouldn't go after it.

She screamed.

"Hush," I said. "I'll fix you a clean one." I walked over to the the board on stumps we were using for a picnic table.

Sadness made me heavy inside. Why did Kiva and I always end up scraping each other raw every time we turned around?

Kiva got up and came to stand beside me. "Preen, listen to me. That's not what I'm saying. What I'm saying is—"

"Erkan's a friend. I owe him a lot and so do you. You shouldn't be jealous because I talked with him for a while."

"You're friends—that's all." Kiva's voice was flat.

"Of course! Erkan's not—I've never thought that way about him." With the memory of how Erkan had looked at me so fresh, I couldn't meet Kiva's eyes.

"All right," he said.

"And even if I had, I'm marrying you at the New Year."

"Wonder what Erkan would think about that." He turned away to stare at the distant crowd around the bull-ring. The clouds of dust above it looked gold in the noon sunshine.

"Besides, I have Sitabi now. I couldn't—"

"Sitabi didn't stop you running off with Rama."

I clenched my fists. "He was her daddy!"

Sitabi heard her name and looked up. "Rama," she said, wrinkling her forehead like she was thinking hard. "I know him."

Kiva glanced down at her with a tight smile. "No, Baby, I don't think so."

I touched his hand. "Everything's different now."

A mountain breeze swirled past and cooled my hot face.

"Because...?" Kiva asked softly.

"Because I've got sense now. Because I've already hurt them too much."

I glanced around the pavilion at the rest of my family. Everyone was trying to look like they couldn't hear us. Mother fussed over the food. Arjun had walked outside and stood with his back to us, hands in his pockets. Sufya whispered to baby Lashmi as she nursed.

The pain in Kiva's eyes told me that wasn't what he wanted to hear.

"And because I love you," I added. "Forget about Erkan."

"Can't. I saw the way he looked at you."

"Why don't you trust me?" Tears made me blink hard.

Kiva moved around the board table and held out his arms. I went to him and he rubbed his hands up and down my back and through my short, rough hair. He didn't say nothing more.

Chapter Seven: Preen

A sharp gust banged the kitchen door open. Dead leaves skittered across the cracked tiles, and the steam from the soup pot blew sideways.

"Arjun?" I called. "Kiva?"

Whoever was outside kicked his boots off.

"Shut that door! It's cold out there."

Kiva marched in, grinning all over his face. He dumped an armful of shopping bags on the table. "I found my bull."

One of the bags fell open and a bottle of fancy lavender-smelling shampoo rolled out. A gift for me. Most likely all the bags held gifts for me.

"Your bull?" I lifted my stirring spoon and tasted the soup. It needed more salt. "You mean the one that trader didn't sell you?"

Kiva wrinkled his nose. "Yes."

"So it's not exactly your bull, is it?" I said, trying not to smile.

"I got the number of the fellow who did buy him. He runs a breeding operation out near Moltoy and he's willing to sell."

"There were other bulls at the fair. You could have—"

"Not as good as that one. He's a Brahma cross, so—"

I held up both hands. "I know, I know. You can tell me all his good points in as much detail as you want—when you've got him."

Kiva grinned. "You can hardly wait, right?"

I turned back to the stove, but he came over and put his arms around me from behind. His beard tickled the back of my neck.

"Stop it!" I slapped at him, laughing. Hard to be sad for long with Kiva in the room. He could share a laugh around quicker than a plate of chocolate biscuits.

"Moltoy's quite a ways," I said. "Got to be half a day's drive, at least. Almost to the Dor border."

"So, time for a road trip. That's actually why I came," he said, suddenly shy. "I thought it might be fun if you came along—if your mother and Arjun say it's all right." Kiva rustled through the bags and pulled out a package of men's socks. "This is mine. Everything else is yours."

He glanced up at me. "You and Sitabi could come with me. We could have a little adventure together as a family."

"But—" I sighed. All the reasons this was a terrible idea flashed through my mind. Most involved Sitabi, temper tantrums, and truck seat cushions soaked with pee.

"Don't worry. My Aunt Desi lives in Moltoy, remember? We'd spend the night at her house," he went on without waiting for an answer. "Pop a biscuit in the gossip's mouth." He crammed the package of socks into his jacket pocket.

A giggle slipped out before I could swallow it.

Kiva lowered his head and looked up at me from under his long eyelashes. "Please?"

I gave the soup a stir. "If Arjun agrees."

"Don't you think it would be fun?"

I took a long breath. Sitabi could wear plastic pants. Every gas station along the way was bound to sell biscuits and treats. "Yes. It'll be fun."

"Great." He spun me around and kissed the tip of my nose. Soup splashed across the floor from the spoon I hadn't had time to drop.

"Look what you made me do!"

He made big fake-sorry eyes and got down his knees with a kitchen rag to clean the mess. Those ragged dreadlocks slid down over his shoulders and hung in his face. "This Friday, then."

"All right."

He tossed the rag into the sink and started for the door. "Is Arjun in the barn? I'd better let him know we'll be using the trailer this weekend."

"It's only 'we' if he agrees."

"Don't worry!"

I stuck my tongue out at him. "Don't tell Sitabi yet, or we'll hear about nothing else until Friday."

Kiva laughed. That big laugh of his warmed me better than the heat from the stove.

He always got what he wanted in the end, one way or another. Getting his way was something he was born with, like the red hair. I'd just have to be happy again someday, because he wanted it so badly.

"By the way, the washer and drier set got delivered for your new kitchen."

"You shouldn't have."

"Well, I did."

I wouldn't be sorry to say goodbye to those big plastic washtubs when Sitabi and I moved into the addition Kiva was building onto his family's house.

"You really shouldn't have." My lips curled.

"Made you smile." He stroked my cheek.

I twined my fingers in his and pushed his hand away. "You act like that's hard to do."

"It's getting easier," he whispered, and dropped a kiss on my nose again. "When we get back from Moltoy, I'll finish painting. Yellow in the kitchen, right?"

"Sure. Dandelion yellow."

"You want it, it's yours. Speaking of which..." he spread his hand toward the pile of bags on the kitchen table.

Since Father was gone, Arjun took charge of making sure Kiva treated me right. But he didn't need to twist Kiva's arm, not even a little bit. Kiva kept bringing me gifts every week or so, even though he'd already paid over half the bride price our families had agreed on.

If he didn't slow down, I wouldn't have room for all the dresses and sweaters and blouses and jeans in my wardrobe. My shelf in the bathroom was piled so high with scented soaps and face creams that I almost caused a little landslide every time I washed.

"Have a look in that black bag and tell me what you think." His eyes still sparkled, but his breath came faster, like he was nervous. "Got samples of five different materials."

"For...?"

"For your wedding dress."

I shook the bag and dumped a pile of silk and taffeta onto the table. "Green?" My voice trembled.

"Yes." He put a finger under my chin and tilted my head up. "It'll bring out the green lights in your eyes."

"The dress should be white." I bit my lower lip to stop it trembling. "Green is for—for virgins. I'm a widow. I should wear white."

He smiled at me with those warm eyes. "Says who?" He picked up a piece with silver threads woven through it. "I like this one. But it's your dress, your day. You pick."

"People will talk."

"Let them! This is our fresh start. Nothing that happened before matters now."

I glanced from the pile of shiny green stuff to his eager, hopeful face and back again. "If you don't care, I..." My voice trailed away. I did care. Rama was my man. My love. Not just something that 'happened.'

Even though my marriage to Rama wasn't valid under Tur Kej law, it hurt that Kiva had chosen green. Did I really want to erase the most important years of my life so far? Did I want to pay what Kiva's idea of a fresh start would cost me in memories—and in truth?

I turned back to the soup pot. Pulled out salt, dumped it in. Tasted again. Too salty now. Tears burned in the back of my nose. "You said you needed to talk to Arjun."

Kiva didn't leave. He stood by the table, fiddling with a piece of green silk. "You don't believe me when I say I don't care what you and Rama did. Preen—" he blew out a long breath. "What am I supposed to do? What do you want from me?"

"I want—"

I wanted him to see I wasn't the girl who used to follow him and Arjun everywhere and laugh at all his jokes. She died with Rama. Someday he'd realize that, and when he did, would he still love me?

"I want to go for a walk. Get some fresh air."

He nodded. "Good idea. We can—"

"Alone."

Chapter Eight: Kiva

"I'm going to take a walk before we eat." Preen turned the gas to Low.

"A walk's a good idea," I said. "We can talk things over."

She turned away. A tuft of hair was sticking out over her ear. I moved close to stroke it down smooth, and so I could see her face.

Her teeth were clenched, but her lips still quivered. What I'd give to see inside her head!

"I'd rather go alone." The pot lid clanged as Preen replaced it.

My heart sank. Before Rama came along and got her pregnant, I thought Preen and I were made for each other. After that, I wasn't so sure.

From the day Arjun took her to Dor to the day I went there myself to bring her home, we didn't speak, not even a phone call. I was too shamed. She must have felt similar, or else she was too took up with Rama. But she was mine—promised to me—so I kept on loving her all the same. I wasn't close to God like Arjun. Didn't pray or read my Bible much, but while Preen was in Dor I prayed every day that God would turn her heart back to me and bring her home. I didn't pray against Rama. I just prayed for Preen.

"Sorry," she said, biting her lip. "I need to be alone for a bit."

"If that's what you want—"

"Yes."

"Sure." Turning, I walked out. In the dark hallway, I slumped against the wall and covered my face.

The first time you get hit, it hurts. It hurts even worse the second time. Maybe around the tenth time you stop feeling it so much. But you never don't feel it at all.

"Kiva?" Preen's voice sounded small and sad. No. I wasn't going back in there. I hated to see her cry. Suddenly I couldn't stand the sound of my own loud breathing or the hair tickling my neck. I dug a string out of my pocket and knotted my dreadlocks up on top of my head.

The sound of the front door slamming broke the silence.

"Dr. Neyrev!" Arjun shouted from out in the yard. "Mrs. Neyrev! Welcome."

What were the Neyrevs doing here? I hadn't heard anybody mention them visiting again. I crossed into the sitting room and went outside to greet them, too.

Dr. Neyrev, his wife, and a skinny Tur fellow in a yellow jacket were coming up the dirt track that ran from our house down to the Duna road. Dr. Neyrev dragged one of those suitcases on wheels and Mrs. Neyrev held something green and spiky in a plastic bag.

When Dr. Neyrev had visited in the spring, he told us he'd barely got past the Public Safety thugs watching his house. How had he managed to make it out of Dor twice? Whatever it was that sent him back there in April must have been worth the risk of spending the rest of his life in a concrete cell—if they let him live.

Arjun ran up and kissed Dr. Neyrev's hand in the Sevian way. Mrs. Neyrev put her whatever-it-was down and threw her arms around Arjun.

I stayed by the door, because the fellow with them was Erkan. Seeing him again sent a little shock of anger down my spine. If he'd come hoping to find Preen, he was going to be disappointed.

Erkan recognized me maybe one second after I recognized him. He set down the canvas bag he was carrying and started back down the track toward the main road.

Dr. Neyrev turned and called after him.

Erkan shouted back something in Sev, waved, and kept going. Not fast. He knew I was watching his every move. I stared after him until that jacket of his was as small as a yellow leaf on the road.

"He was in a hurry," Arjun said.

Mrs. Neyrev laughed. "Yes, Erkan actually had a client waiting, but the bus wasn't coming by until four, so he insisted on helping us get here first."

Arjun went to get the bag Erkan had dropped. I took Dr. Neyrev's suitcase and Mrs. Neyrev's plastic bag. Inside was some kind of plant with thick leaves that oozed jelly from the broken parts.

"My aloe plant," she said. "Poor thing. It looks as battered as I feel."

I poked it gently, thinking of all she'd been through the past couple of years. "Will it live?"

Her weak laugh turned into a cough. "Oh, yes. I'm not sure it's possible to kill an aloe plant."

***

"I should have brought Oksana with me when I came in April." Dr. Neyrev sipped his tea like it tasted bitter. He coughed and wiped his mouth. He looked bad—worse than in the spring. He'd gotten so thin his nose was too big for his face and his bony shoulders sagged. "But she simply refused to leave Dor permanently until I did."

Mrs. Neyrev clicked her tongue. "You couldn't have expected me to abandon you!"

"I was in the middle of helping with negotiations between the Rais of Dor and the new government," Dr. Neyrev said. "They're trying to determine what's to be done with the Rayad members still in Camp Peace, and I must say it isn't going well."

He took another sip of tea and put the cup down in the exact center of his saucer. "There are still so many in the camp. One European League vote away from being handed over to Simon Nevin." His voice got rough. "It's hard, so hard, knowing that and knowing there's nothing I can do about it."

We all sat quiet for a minute.

Dr. Neyrev ran his tongue over his lips. "Then we got word that I would most likely be arrested again. The old weapons-smuggling charge."

Across the table, Arjun shook his head. He was gentle to a fault, but when he first heard Dr. Neyrev had been charged with smuggling weapons for Rayad, he'd looked ready to tear Riverside Prison down with his bare hands.

"So how did you get out of Dor?" I asked.

Dr. Neyrev pressed his thin lips together. "Well, there's more than one way out of Dor. It's not as if I don't know any smugglers. However—" he stopped. His eyes flashed from Arjun to me and back again.

The tea I just drank turned cold in my stomach.

"Something happened?" Arjun asked softly.

"I don't want to alarm you, but when we met our smugglers at the point we agreed on, I was more than a little surprised to find that I recognized one of them from less happy circumstances." Dr. Neyrev sighed.

I waited. Being forced to run for your life with nothing except your clothes and your wife's ugly plant didn't seem like a happy circumstance to me.

"What do you mean?" Arjun looked confused.

I squeezed the edges of my chair. Somehow I already knew what Dr. Neyrev was going to say. "One of the smugglers—the owner of the vehicle that brought us out of Dor Province, in fact—was Sanjit."

Ever since Erkan showed up at the autumn fair, I'd had a feeling that Sanjit would too, sooner or later. The nastiest piece in the puzzle of Preen's life.

Arjun's mouth dropped open. "What? No."

"Unfortunately, yes. He's helped quite a few wanted people escape Dor. Smuggling seems to come naturally to him."

"Where is he now?" Arjun asked.

"Probably in Duna. That's where he left us, anyway. He's from Tur Fen, but he mentioned that he has relatives near Duna. I think he's planning to visit them."

"What if he's lying? What if he's really here to look for Preen?"

"He said nothing about that," Dr. Neyrev picked up his tea glass and looked at the brown shreds in the bottom.

"Why would he?" I moved to get up.

Preen's mother put her hand on my arm.

"Peter, don't you think—" Mrs. Neyrev began.

"I imagine he won't be in the area long," her husband interrupted. "It's nothing to worry about. He'll most likely return to Dor soon. After all, his profession is quite lucrative these days—but I thought you ought to know. Just in case."

Just in case? Fear and anger both ran through me. "He dropped you off down in Duna, right? And you didn't tell him anything about us?"

Dr. Neyrev's forehead wrinkled. "Of course not. Why would I do that?" He started coughing again.

Mrs. Neyrev leaned over and handed him a handkerchief.

He coughed harder. Tears started in his eyes.

"I'll get you some water," Arjun said.

Nobody who didn't know Arjun like I did would guess he was as worried as me. Even when things got bad, the smile on his round face rarely faded.

Mrs. Neyrev's chair screeched as she pulled it closer to her husband. The sound almost made me jump out of my skin.

She winced. "Sorry."

Dr. Neyrev's breath rattled in his throat. He gulped the water Arjun handed him. "Had pneumonia. In Dor Fen. Prison." He shook his head like he was trying to clear it. "Now this. Cough. Won't go away."

Mrs. Neyrev rubbed her husband's shoulders. "Is there somewhere Peter could lie down for a bit? It's been a long day."

"The guest room's always ready for you," Preen's mother said, twisting the end of her long braid between her fingers. Her mouth smiled, but her eyes looked distant. Like me, she was thinking about Sanjit, and what could happen if—

"By the way, where is Preen?" Mrs. Neyrev asked. "We're looking forward to seeing her and Sitabi again."

That was when it hit me like a steer's hoof in the gut. My Preen was out there somewhere, walking on the hills, or on the road. Alone.

What if she decided to head toward Duna? I couldn't stand the thought of Sanjit within a mile of her. Or a hundred miles. Not sure how I felt about him being in the same world with her.

I stood so fast all the tea glasses on the table rattled. "Be right back."

Chapter Nine: Preen

Just as I pulled my heavy sweater off the chair back, Mother walked into the kitchen. "The Neyrevs are here," she said. "You and Sitabi will need to move back into my room. Actually, you'd better move Sitabi now—she's asleep on the bed in there and I need to change the sheets."

I swallowed hard. Crying over Kiva's thickheadedness would have to wait. "Mrs. Neyrev came too?"

"Yes. They're here to stay this time, I think." She picked up a rag and swished it back and forth across the wooden table, knocking crumbs from Sitabi's breakfast onto the floor.

"Here on the farm, you mean?" We weren't exactly rattling around loose in the house as it was. But Dr. Neyrev was my father's dearest friend. If they planned to live in Tur Kej, where else would they go?

"Unless they find a place in Duna they like better, yes." Mother headed over to the stove, dipped a spoon into the soup and made a face. "How much salt did you put in this?"

I shrugged. "Enough."

"They had to use a smuggler to help them get out of Dor," she added. "One of those Rayad gun-runners, probably. Why don't you throw some of those tinned beans into the soup? Make it go farther."

"Sure."

Crossing the kitchen, she opened the pantry cupboard and set two tins of black beans on the counter. "Any bread left?"

"I don't think so."

"Well, we'll have to make do." Mother's long skirt swished as she fussed around, peeking into more cupboards. "What else? The guest sheets...and I'd better put another blanket out to air."

"I hope Dr. Neyrev's better than he was in the spring," I said.

She stopped. For a moment, her hands hung limp by her sides. "I don't know. He looks drained, like your father did near the end. But Mrs. Neyrev seems well. She's excited to see you and Sitabi."

Sitabi had been a baby the last time Mrs. Neyrev saw her, when we were still living in Dor.

"I'd better get that room ready. Would you—" Mother pointed at the tea kettle.

"Get Sufya to do it. She's around, isn't she?"

The sound of Lashmi squalling drifted in from Arjun and Sufya's room.

"She's busy." Mother frowned. "Is everything all right?"

"I'm fine." I bit my lip. "Just a headache. I've been in the kitchen all morning."

That was true, but my head didn't hurt from spending time in the stuffy kitchen. "I was planning to go for a walk when the soup was done."

"Preen, we have guests."

"Please." Tears started leaking out under my eyelids. I couldn't go out into the sitting room and smile and talk and serve tea while Kiva stared me down with those sad, hopeful eyes. I just couldn't.

Mother sighed. "If you must."

I started for the back door.

"Preen—"

"Yes?" The doorknob chilled my fingers.

"If something's wrong, you'll tell me, won't you?"

Probably not.

Sitabi appeared in the kitchen doorway, rubbing her rosy face. "Mama? Mama? I woke up!"

My turn to sigh. "Yes, you did. Want a biscuit?"

"Are you going outside? I want to come."

"It's cold."

"Please." She clasped her hands to her chest. "Please please please!"

"All right. But you'll have to ride."

I put on my sweater and hoisted Sitabi onto my back. Pulling Mother's red shawl off the hook by the door, I wrapped it around us and knotted it across my chest, so it supported her like a sling. Her soft little body fit perfect against mine.

We creaked down the back steps and started up the path toward the hill pasture. The air smelled like rain. Layers of clouds covered the sky, heavy and gray. The wind hissed through clumps of grass, and pushed the breath back down my throat.

Sitabi ducked her head against my shoulder. "Coooold!" she squealed.

I reached back and ruffled her hair. "You asked to come. Want to go back to Grandma?"

"No."

"Don't make a fuss, then."

Out on the hills, my thoughts came easier. Things that confused me started to make sense. Things that drove me wild when I was inside, in the chatter and shouting and greasy smells, didn't seem so bad when I could walk under the sky. If I was all alone, I'd sometimes spread out my arms and run.

The wind blew my hair straight up on my head as we climbed the hill behind the farmhouse. As my feet took us up the narrow cow-trail, my mind ran back to Kiva and our almost-fight in the kitchen.

Kiva couldn't see why he'd hurt me, because in his mind, my marriage to Rama wasn't nothing but a two-year fling with a gangster boyfriend. Buying me green fabric was his way of saying he forgave me for it, and was ready to start again where we'd left off. "Look, Mama!" Sitabi shouted in my ear.

A man on a lanky white horse had crested the hill off to our right. I stopped. Some of our neighbors sometimes cut across our pastureland to reach the Duna road, but they didn't own any white horses as far as I knew.

The man rode loose and easy, like he'd grown up riding. A ray of sun shot down between the clouds and flashed off something metal in his topknot of dreadlocks. When he saw us, he waved.

Everything inside me screamed, 'Run,' but I didn't. Even without Sitabi tied on my back, I couldn't outrun a horse. So I stood still, shaking all over, and waited for Sanjit to ride up.

"Preen!" Sanjit called as he got close. "Preen Enda!"

At the sound of his voice, the air got so thick it hurt to breathe. I wrapped my arms across my chest. The bruises from his kicks had showed yellow on my ribs for weeks afterwards.

"What are you doing here?" The wind blew the words out of my mouth, back down toward the barn and farmhouse. He murmured something to the horse and pulled the reins.

"I came to talk with you." His voice cracked like he was nervous. "So, this is your place. Your family owns more pastureland than I expected."

No need to tell him most of it was rented from the Manjalis. My eyes locked on the pistol bulge in the leather jacket that used to be Rama's. "How did you—?" I swallowed. "How did you find us?"

"Wasn't hard," he said. "Half the people in Duna know Dr. Neyrev, and half of those know that he stays at the Rastikars' farm when he's in Tur Kej."

I opened my mouth, but no words came.

The soft, wet sound of Sitabi sucking her thumb right against my ear set my heart galloping. I shouldn't have let her come. What if Sanjit hurt my little girl?

My pulse pounded in my ears as I studied his face—silver earrings, wide mouth, scruffy beard. Just like I saw it in my dreams sometimes. "If you—if you try anything—they're right down the hill." I swallowed again to wet my dry mouth. "My dad. All my brothers. If I scream, they'll come running and you'll get a facefull of birdshot." I backed away, caught my heel on a tuft of grass and almost fell.

"Relax, Preen. You act like I'm going to hurt you."

"Is that strange?"

"No—no." His eyes slid away from mine.

"That's why we need to talk. Listen, Preen. Can you let what happened in Dor stay there? What I did was terrible, I know that. So I'm asking—" He ran his tongue across his lower lip. "I'm asking you to forgive me."

My mouth fell open. "What?"

"I understand, it's a lot to ask, but—"

"You rode up here to say sorry?"

"Yes."

Behind him, the setting sun came out of the clouds, throwing his face into shadow.

I laughed. Couldn't help it, I was so giddy with shock and relief. A minute ago I thought I was going to die.

Sitabi bounced on my back, stretching one hand toward the horse's nose. The shawl's fringe tickled my neck as she squirmed. "Mama!"

"Quiet, Baby Girl." I pulled her hand down and looked up at Sanjit. "I don't understand."

He unzipped his jacket partway and pulled a rubber-banded roll of money out of the inner pocket. "I brought this for you. To help smooth things over a little." He grinned nervously, showing the gaps where his wolf-teeth used to be. "I'm sorry I took things so far. I really am. What Rama did wasn't your fault."

I didn't know what to say, so I stood there with my mouth open. I'd already forgiven Sanjit for what he'd done, but that didn't mean I wanted to see him again. That didn't mean I had to trust him, did it? My nose ring felt cold as ice against my upper lip.

He leaned forward in his squeaky saddle and held out a roll of money. "Take it."

My hand went out like it wasn't part of me, and he pressed it into my palm. "Why?" I could hardly speak above a whisper.

He smiled again, too wide to look innocent. "A token of...friendship. We're going to be neighbors."

My head spun. The things he was saying didn't make any sense. Either he'd gone crazy, or I had.

"Neighbors shouldn't carry on quarrels," he added. "Don't you agree?"

"Neighbors?" I repeated, like an idiot.

Sanjit nodded. "My father doesn't own any land. My uncle doesn't have any sons. He's been sick for a long time, and he's getting worse—might not last out the year. When he's gone his farm comes to me. It's about half a kilometer south of here, toward Duna."

I gasped. He had to be talking about old Manish Sind's place. Never in a million years would I have guessed that Manish was Sanjit's uncle. Manish was a brittle, grumpy old man—harmless. "You're a Sind?"

"On my father's side."

"That can't be true!"

"It is." The silver beads in his dreadlocks glittered when he bowed his head. The horse snorted and scraped the ground with one hoof, shaking its warm smell toward me. Sanjit stroked its neck. "Listen. You and I have a lot in common."

"No, we don't."

"Oh yes, we do. The only real difference is, you didn't get the chance to hide your mistakes." He jerked his chin toward Sitabi. "She'd be cute if she didn't look so much like her father."

A lot of nasty things I could say suddenly came to mind.

"I'd like to spend the rest of my life in peace, up here in these hills." Sanjit tipped his head back and looked up at the streaky sky. "I don't want any rocks from the past breaking my windows."

"I'm cold. Let's go home," Sitabi whined. "Let's go."

I squeezed her tiny fingers. "In a minute."

"Look at it this way," he said. "The old Sanjit, the one who went to Dor to fight for Ray ad, is dead and gone. Nothing he did there matters up here. This Sanjit—" he touched his chest, "Will soon inherit his uncle's farm. I want my life. You want yours. No reason we can't both be happy, right?"

"You said you'd make me pay for what Rama did."

"That's finished now. I'm starting over. Can't you get that into your head?"

"So you've forgiven Rama?" My sweaty hand dampened the roll of money as I squeezed it.

For a long minute he stared at me, like the question had shocked all the words out of him. "Forgiven Rama for selling out Askar and Mosin?" His lips curled away from his teeth. "What do you think? If I could choose between giving him what he had coming and my uncle's thirty head of cattle—it wouldn't take me a second to choose." He snapped his fingers. "Not one second."

"I'm sorry," I whispered. "So sorry Rama got your brothers killed."

"Rama ended so easy—went off to sleep with you beside him, holding his hand. God's justice is a joke." Sanjit blinked hard, and scraped the back of his hand across his face. I looked away. If God gave Sanjit and me what we deserved, we wouldn't neither of us be alive anymore.

Chapter Ten: Preen

"Uncle Manish's farm should have been split three ways," Sanjit said. "For Askar, Mosin and me."

"They tortured Rama for days before he broke," I said. "You know that, don't you?" His eyes went wide. "Forget it!" he yelled. The horse shied, and he had to grab its mane to steady himself. He clicked his tongue to soothe it. "Easy, now. Hush. Forget it, forget it," he muttered, patting its neck.

The horse bobbed its head up and down, jingling the bridle.

Sitabi began to whimper. She dropped her head on my shoulder.

I tightened the knot in the red shawl.

"The dead are dead." Sanjit spoke in jerks, as jumpy as the horse. "It doesn't matter now. Everything's new."

"What happens when your family finds out about how you sold girls in Klim and Camp Peace?"

His eyes narrowed. "Please don't go starting ugly rumors, Preen." My name sounded poisonous, the way he said it. He leaned toward me, so close his sickly cologne overpowered the good smells of horse and saddle leather. "Why should you talk about what I did in Dor, anyway? It's over now."

"I'm not the only one who knows." My voice sounded as shrill as Sitabi's. "Kiva knows what you were up to there. So does Arjun. And—" I almost let Erkan's name fall. Maybe Sanjit didn't know Erkan had escaped Dor, too.

"I'm sure you'll figure out a way to keep them quiet."

I stared at the ground. Down at the barn, the wind banged a shutter or something back and forth, back and forth.

I nodded. But I wanted so bad to tell him what I thought of him that it almost made me choke. "If you think owning land will help you sleep easy—"

"There's a house," Sanjit said, like he hadn't heard me. "A big barn. A good-sized herd." He ticked off each thing on his dirty fingers. "With some work, I'll have enough to retire on in a couple of years, so that's what I'm planning to do. It's so beautiful here," he added softly, like he was talking to himself. "People can really breathe this air."

For a long time, neither of us said anything. Only the horse moved.

Sanjit broke the silence. "Not everybody gets a second chance. Let's not ruin ours." He nodded at me and rode off in the same direction he'd come.

As the thud of hoof-beats died away, a mass of clouds slid over the sun. The sky turned a sad orange-gold.

"It's freezing, Baby Girl," I said. "We'd better go. Don't want you to catch a chill." I threw the roll of money as far as I could and stumbled down the path toward our house on shaky legs. My teeth chattered. My head spun. So Sanjit was going to own the farm next over? Short of everything that had already happened, I couldn't imagine anything worse.

Sitabi bounced against my back, kicking her feet. One of her socks went flying.

When I stooped to pick it up, I lost my balance and fell. I sat back, pulled my knees to my chest and rubbed the places where rocks had scraped them.

Sitabi started crying. I'd scared her, dropping so sudden and not getting up, but I couldn't help it.

"Preen!" Kiva shouted from below. "Are you all right?" He came racing up the path. "I've been looking everywhere for you!"

"I'm fine," I choked out.

"What happened? What's wrong?" He dropped to his knees beside Sitabi and me and pulled us both into his chest. His heart was pounding even harder than mine.

"Sanjit was here," I whispered.

Kiva sucked in his breath. "What did he—"

I pulled away, feeling foolish for being so scared. "He didn't do nothing. We just talked."

"That's all?"

"Yes." Sitabi started tugging on his arm, so he lifted her out of the shawl sling and cuddled her.

"Sanjit is Manish Sind's oldest nephew," I said. "Can you believe it? Sanjit."

Kiva's eyebrows drew together. "That means he'll likely get the Sind farm when Manish goes."

I nodded. "That's mostly what we talked about. He says he's going to settle down and be a farmer."

"A fellow like him can't just 'settle down,'" Kiva said. "If he comes here, it won't be long before he's got a setup in Duna like he had in Dor—with all the refugees from Dor, he'll probably even find old customers."

"But he said—"

"If he doesn't, it won't be for lack of trying."

"But maybe he won't." I untied the red shawl and handed it to Kiva, who tucked it around Sitabi.

"The last thing he wants is his family finding out how he made his money in Dor," I said. "He wouldn't dare try it again here."

"No." Kiva shook his head. "Someone like Sanjit doesn't know the meaning of shame."

"He said he wants a fresh start." My throat closed on the last words. God gave me another chance. Who was I to say Sanjit didn't deserve one, too? "He told me he was sorry for—for what happened in the spring."

Kiva's fingers brushed my cheek. Gently, he turned my head so I had to look him in the face. "Do you believe him?"

"Yes." I wanted to look away, but those green eyes held mine. "I...I think so."

"You believe he meant it?"

"Maybe. Either way, I've forgiven him for what he did to me. God can change people, even the worst people."

"Why did God have to go and change Sanjit?" Kiva muttered. He looked past me, up the slope that was almost gray now that the sun had gone. "So we welcome him as our new neighbor and make him part of our community?" he said slowly. "No. We can't do that."

The grayness settled inside me, and made my stomach cold. "Aren't we supposed to? He agreed he'd done wrong."

Kiva didn't say anything, just sat there, running his tongue across his lower lip.

Rama used to do the very same thing when he was thinking hard.

I waited. Without Sitabi snuggled against my back, the wind cut right through my sweater like it was cotton instead of double-knit wool. I pulled the ends of my sleeves down around my fingers. "Forgive your enemies. It's in the Bible lots of times. Forgive your enemies. So that's what we have to do." I clenched my teeth to keep them from rattling together.

"You're right," Kiva said. "But I think you're also wrong."

Rain started spitting down, fat drops that made near-black spots on his shirt and the red shawl.

Kiva scrambled to his feet, shifted Sitabi onto his hip and helped me stand. "Let's get back down to the house. We can talk later. No sense in sitting out here getting soaked."

***

In the front hall, Kiva handed Sitabi back to me.

The rain had chilled her cheeks almost as cold as the little silver hoops in her ears. I rubbed a corner of the shawl over her face and head until she batted it away.

Kiva shook raindrops out of his topknot and tossed his boots into a basket by the door. Then he headed for the sitting room.

"Staying for dinner?" I asked. The brown smell of bean soup was so thick in the hall you could almost see it.

"Why not? I'll add some water to my soup if the pot looks low."

I made a face. "You can eat my share. I'm not hungry."

He clicked his tongue. "Preen, you're never hungry anymore."

"You sound like my mother."

"So?" He shrugged. "If you don't want people to worry so much about you, then eat more."

Since Rama died and I came back from Dor alone, eating made my stomach hurt. But I didn't care. Nothing tasted as good as it used to.

"I want to hear what Arjun and Dr. Neyrev think about Sanjit," Kiva said.

"I already know what they think about Sanjit."

He gave me a quick, tense smile. "I mean about him coming to live here."

Chapter Eleven: Preen

After we ate, I got Sitabi ready for bed.

The others gathered in the front room, except Mother, who was leading the women's prayer meeting in Duna that evening.

Sitabi asked for a lullaby, but I wanted to hear what the men down the hall were talking about. We compromised by sitting right by the bedroom door while I whispered her a song. All I could hear was a low murmur, except when Mrs. Neyrev said, "He's still very young." Was she talking about Sanjit?

When Sitabi nodded off, I laid her down in the middle of Mother's bed and pulled the blanket up to her chin. She went to sleep easy—the cold walk and hot dinner probably helped.

"Sanjit ran a large prostitution ring in Klim," Dr. Neyrev was saying as I walked into the front room. "He'd have no trouble finding someone to take over the dirtier aspects of his business if he wanted to back off and take a more...administrative...role."

"Exactly," Kiva broke in. "There's no way he's really done. The Sind place has been falling apart for years. He's going to need money to get it up and running again." He leaned back against the wall to the right of the fireplace and folded his arms. The orange glow from the hearth made sharp shadows across his face.

Dr. Neyrev took off his glasses. His pale eyes had started to water. "You're right. I doubt he'll give it up completely. Too profitable." He sighed. "Shortly after I was released from prison, back in the early spring, I spoke with a few of the young women involved with him, and—" He broke off and squinted up at me.

Nobody said what we were all thinking. I could have been one of those young women. If not for Erkan's courage and quick thinking, I would have been.

Mrs. Neyrev broke the silence. "Come sit." She waved to me. "You should be part of this conversation."

Arjun and Kiva exchanged a worried look, like they were scared I'd shrivel up and die if I heard Sanjit's name too much.

I went to take one of the wooden chairs by the hearth, but Kiva nudged Arjun over and patted the spot on the bench between them. When I sat down, he put his arm around me.

"Preen, what exactly did Sanjit tell you?" Dr. Neyrev asked. He rubbed his glasses on his sleeve and put them back on.

I eased away from Kiva a little bit. Snuggling with him was cozy, but the warm room brought the manure reek out of his clothes.

"He told me he was done with all that," I said into the thick silence. "He says he's sorry for the trouble he caused and...he's...he's done." I twisted the cuff of my sweater around my fingers.

Dr. Neyrev adjusted his glasses on his nose. "You don't sound very convinced."

I stared at the floor. Much easier to follow the pattern of knots and cracks in the floorboards than meet his eyes. How convinced did I have to be to make me forgiving him real? "If he'd wanted to hurt me, he easily could have, up on the hill. But he didn't. Not me or Sitabi."

"That's true." The worried creases deepened in Dr. Neyrev's forehead. "But I'm not sure that means he's a reformed character, either." Knowing Dr. Neyrev was worried lifted a weight off my heart. Maybe it wasn't wrong to be wary. Maybe just because Sanjit said he was sorry didn't mean he had to be my new best friend.

"He offered me money," I added in a small voice. "I threw it away."

Kiva scowled. "Of all the—"

The rickety bench creaked as Arjun leaned forward. "That was a stupid thing for Sanjit to do, but I think it's clear that he didn't come to pick a fight with us. I see no reason why we should start one with him."

"I didn't say anything about starting a fight," Kiva said. "But the fellow's slime, and here he is hoping to buy Preen off—"

"Preen's forgiven him for what he did. If she can, we can," Arjun said.

"You're missing the point," Kiva said. "I didn't say we can't forgive him. We're not out to wreck his life—but that doesn't mean we want a former pimp and kidnapper as our nearest neighbor."

"What gives us the right to say that he doesn't deserve a chance to start over?" Arjun asked.

Kiva slapped the bench in frustration. "If he really wants to start over, let him do it somewhere else."

"Where else is he inheriting land?" Arjun's eyebrows went up.

"So? He can sell the farm and set up again wherever he wants to. I say we give him a choice—he moves, or we bring a complaint against him to the Rais."

I grabbed Kiva's hand. "No! We can't do that." Whether he was truly sorry or not, Sanjit was a cornered snake. The last thing I wanted was for Kiva to go up and poke him.

Sanjit's words to me kept running through my head. 'Not everyone gets a second chance. Let's not ruin ours.'

When I closed my eyes, I saw Kiva sprawled on his back in the house-yard, his fingers grabbing for the bloody holes in his shirt. I saw Sanjit standing over him, aiming his gun at me.

Arjun's round face had lost color. Could he also be afraid of what might happen if we tried to get Sanjit arrested? But if we left him alone, no reason he wouldn't leave us alone, too.

"We can't bring a complaint," I whispered.

Kiva pulled me a little closer and leaned his head against mine. "Yes, we can. The thought of Sanjit living close by scares you to death. I can see it in your face."

The room got quiet. A log fell apart with a sharp crackle and a puff of sparks flew up the chimney. The noise made me jump.

"You want him gone, Preenalaya, he's gone." Kiva's voice held a dark edge I'd never heard before.

Was it wrong that I wanted Sanjit gone? I swallowed something like grit mixed with salty tears. "I don't want to be the reason he doesn't get his second chance, because I'm scared. That's not right."

"You know what else is not right? That you have to live in the shadow of the man who kidnapped you," Kiva said. "That we'll be raising our daughter a few fields away from a woman-stealer."

"I said I forgave him, so..."

"Preen, that's not what forgiveness means!" He took my hand and sqeezed it.

I traced a crack in the floorboard with my toe. "If I've really forgiven him, I don't think I should bring a complaint against him and maybe make him lose his land. What kind of forgiveness is that?"

Kiva tipped his head back and let out all his breath in a long sigh."You don't understand."

"She's telling you how she feels," Dr. Neyrev said softly. "In my experience, it's best to listen."

Arjun looked up at the plaster ceiling. "That farm has been Sind land for a hundred years. They're good people, the Sinds. Most of them."

"So? You know what they say about rotten apples."

"Out of respect for his family, I think we should wait," Arjun said.

Kiva ignored him. "If Sanjit was Manish's son, he'd inherit, no questions asked. Even the Rais's Council couldn't rule against it. That's Tur Kej law. But..." Kiva glanced at Dr. Neyrev and his wife.

"I'm familiar with that law," Dr. Neyrev said. "Go on."

"Since Sanjit is only his nephew, if someone were to bring a formal complaint, the Rais might decide that he can't inherit the land." Kiva took a long breath and glanced sideways at Mrs. Neyrev. "Maybe you can interpret for her?"

She smiled. "It's all right. I mostly understand."

Kiva went on. "If the Council rules against him, Sanjit would be passed over for a more deserving relative."

Dr. Neyrev cleared his throat. "But this isn't exactly a property dispute, or a question of who's the rightful heir, is it? What kind of complaint do you plan to bring?"

"Kidnapping." Kiva's jaw tightened on the word.

Mrs. Neyrev nodded, but she didn't say anything.

Arjun sighed. "Slow down, Kiva."

The bench rocked as Kiva jumped to his feet. "What do you mean, 'Slow down?' We're talking about the fellow who took Preen!"

I bit the inside of my cheek until the pain made sparks behind my eyes. For a second I was back in Dor, lying facedown on the sidewalk with Sanjit standing over me, pressing a gun to the back of my head. But Sanjit hadn't shamed his family the way I had—at least not so they knew about it. What business did I have hoping to be forgiven if he wasn't?

Kiva started pacing the room. He tossed another log into the fireplace, then went and jerked the window curtains closed.

Dr. Neyrev pushed his chair back. He got up, wincing, and went over to Kiva, who stood by the window where Mrs. Neyrev had set her aloe plant. "I can see why you're concerned," Dr. Neyrev said. "I am, too. It would be better not to have a man like Sanjit in the area." He laid one hand on Kiva's shoulder. "But I don't think any of us want to see him hanged."

"Of course not. But—" Kiva's face flushed red.

Maybe he was right and I was confused about what forgiveness meant, but one thing I knew for sure—it didn't mean Sanjit dangling from a rope.

Kiva glanced from Dr. Neyrev to me and back again. "He's from Tur Fen. Our Rais can't have him executed."

"True, but when he's sent back to Tur Fen, do you think it's likely his own Rais will just let him go, knowing he's a kidnapper?"

"We'll get him for prostitution, then. That's not a capital offense."

"You'll accuse him of prostituting multiple women but conveniently forget to mention that he also kidnapped your fiancee?" Dr. Neyrev sighed. "Don't you see? It's all or nothing."

Kiva took a long breath. "All right, then."

"So forget it," I said softly.

"How many witnesses would you need to present a criminal complaint of this kind to the Rais?" Dr. Neyrev asked.

"Two," Kiva said. "Except Preen wasn't eighteen when it happened, so she'll need an extra adult to back up her testimony. So three. But that's easy. Me. Preen. Arjun." He held up three fingers.

"Kiva—!" I was so mad I jumped up, too. Why did he even bother asking me what I thought if he didn't let me talk, and when I did talk, he didn't listen?

"No. Not me," Arjun said.

Kiva took a step toward him. "What did you say?" Shock and anger turned that handsome face of his ugly.

"I'm not going to testify against Sanjit." Arjun's voice was still soft, but his eyes didn't leave Kiva's.

"What do you mean? What's wrong with you?"

Deep down, I'd known what Arjun would say, but Kiva looked like Arjun had kicked his feet out from under him.

"I don't think God gave me the right to do anything that would put someone else in danger," Arjun said.

He wasn't just talking. Arjun had been treated bad so many times when we lived in Dor. I'd seen him pushed around, called names, even thrown out of a store once— and he'd never raised a hand to anybody. I still didn't know if it made me proud or ashamed of him.

Kiva took a long breath. "Not ever? Not for any reason?"

"I can't think of a reason," Arjun answered.

Dr. Neyrev nodded thoughtfully.

Mrs. Neyrev looked like she had a pain inside. She reached up to tuck some loose strands of hair back under her scarf. Her fingers trembled so much she almost couldn't do it.

"So you believe Sanjit's story?" Kiva asked.

Arjun shrugged. "For now, yes. All we know is that Sanjit told Preen he's turning his life around."

"Sanjit tried to sell your sister!" Kiva yelled, throwing his arms wide. The black patterns on them looked like strange scars in the dim light.

Arjun sat so still that every thing he said seemed extra-important. "Yes."

"If I didn't know you better, I'd call you a coward."

Arjun said nothing.

"So that's what we're going to do." Kiva's voice shook, he was so mad. "Give the woman-stealer a chance. You say you don't want to hurt anybody." He planted himself in front of Arjun and leaned toward him. "I hope you don't live to regret it."

I squeezed my clenched fists together in my lap. Arjun had to be right. If I'd listened to my brother before, the worst things in my life would never have happened. But the best things wouldn't have, either.

Kiva turned to me. "If Sanjit comes after you again, there's nothing I won't do to stop him," he said.

Arjun smiled. "So that's why you left your shotgun in the car that day you decided to become a human shield?"

Kiva stared at him for a second. The stony look on his face melted into an embarrassed grin. "Whatever."

"Preen, what do you think should be done about Sanjit?" Dr. Neyrev asked.

"He should be able to settle down on his family farm if he wants to." I folded my arms across my chest to hold in the part of me that was crying, 'No! Not here. Not in my one safe place.'

What did it mean to forgive somebody? Did it mean you had to trust him again, no matter what he did? Did it mean he was free to do it again?

"Let's leave him be for now," I said.

Arjun nodded. His smile was just like our father's—except for the gaps in his teeth that still made me sick if I thought about them too much.

I looked up at Kiva. Too bad I couldn't borrow his quick tongue now and again.

"That's really what you want?" Kiva asked.

Suddenly I was bone-weary, like at the end of a long hike. "Yes."

Kiva opened his mouth to say something more, but changed his mind. He started pulling pieces of matted hair out of his topknot and winding them around his fingers.

Dr. Neyrev gave me a long, steady look. "All right, then. Sanjit gets another chance."

Chapter Twelve: Kiva

I was about to tell Preen all the reasons why not prosecuting Sanjit was the wrong choice, but Arjun leaned forward, holding up his hand. "If she thinks it's right for Sanjit to go free, it's not our place to try and change her mind. If he turns out to be lying, then we'll do what we need to do when the time comes." He gave her an encouraging smile.

She didn't smile back.

I could have punched him. "Look at your sister!" I shouted. "Forget your ideals and look at her. Is that the face of someone who's telling us what she really wants?"

Preen wrapped her thin arms across her stomach, squeezing her elbows. I went over to her and pulled her into my arms. "You don't think you deserve justice, that's what it is. You think that Sanjit shouldn't have to answer for what he did to you because—"

"I don't think he's going to do anything bad here because he's hoping for that farm. He wants to live up where people can breathe. That's what he said." Preen's voice shook.

The wind that had been blowing high all evening around the Rastikars' farmhouse came humming down the chimney. Ash flakes puffed into the sitting room. A coal jumped out of the fireplace and smoulderered on the rag rug near the hearth.

Arjun put out his foot and smothered it under his thick leather slipper.

"My dear, there's no hurry to make a decision," Mrs. Neyrev said from her place at the table beside her husband. "Whether or not you decide you wish to prosecute him, either way, it's an enormous step to take."

Dr. Neyrev coughed into his napkin. That juniper smoke must have been catching him in the back of his throat.

"I understand your position, Kiva," he nodded at me, "and knowing what I know about Sanjit, I have a feeling that lodging a complaint with the Rais would be the wisest course of action. That being said," he turned toward Preen, "I admire your desire to give Sanjit a period of grace. However..." He paused so long I thought he'd decided not to say anything more. Then he sighed and folded his hands on the tabletop, crumpling the napkin between them. "Preen, if you change your mind, I'd be glad to testify against Sanjit for your case. Even though Oksana and I happen to owe him our lives, I'd do it."

Preen put a hand on the edge of the door frame like she needed to steady herself and stared at him, confusion written all over her face. "Why?"

Dr. Neyrev cleared his throat. "As I mentioned, I had the opportunity to speak to some of the young women who were selling themselves out of Camp Peace and Klim. For flour and tea and bags of potatoes. Why would I not witness against one of the people responsible, if the opportunity arose?"

"But I thought..." Preen ran a finger up and down the knotty pattern in the doorframe. "I thought you'd have to agree with Arjun."

"Don't you mean he'd have to agree with me?" Dr. Neyrev gave her his squinty-eyed smile. "Since I'm considerably older, I should be the one originating the ideas, shouldn't I?"

Arjun laughed.

For a bit the tension running between us all got less. I felt the ease in my shoulders and the back of my neck.

Preen stood in the doorway, part in the dark hallway, part in the firelight. The skin under her eyes looked dark as bruises. "Sanjit came here for a new start. If God's given him another chance, I can't be the one to take it away."

Dr. Neyrev nodded.

"You didn't report the man who killed your son," Preen said.

"I wanted to see justice done," Dr. Neyrev slipped off his glasses again and started rubbing them with the corner of the napkin. "But it was a very complicated situation."

"I thought you didn't care about justice," Preen said. "Just forgiveness, no matter what."

"I don't believe they're mutually exclusive," Dr. Neyrev said, just before I said, "No reason you can't have both."

"But how are you supposed to know that?" Preen asked. "How do you decide?"

"There's a difference between the rash action of a man caught in a bad situation—like Taj in the alley with my son—and the ongoing abuse perpetrated by a man who chose to insert himself into the bad situation—like Sanjit in Camp Peace." He kept rubbing and rubbing those clean lenses with his napkin. "Does that make sense?"

"I think so," Preen said.

"You're not the only person Sanjit has hurt," I told her. "Just because you've forgiven him doesn't mean he won't have to face what he's got coming."

"What about when I hurt you?" She spoke so soft I wouldn't have heard if I didn't have an arm around her. "You forgave me each and every time."

I stared down at her for a minute, surprised. "That was completely different."

"Why?"

"Because—" I saw my Preen coming down the cattle trail with Rama, hands cupped beneath her growing belly, walking past me like I wasn't there. The memory made me hot with shame. Sick with that everlasting pain. The longer I chewed all the 'whys' I wanted to ask her, the worse they tasted. Stop, I told myself. It's done. Leave it be. "Because it was. You loved Rama, so you went with him. That's all."

"Preen," Dr. Neyrev coughed. He probably hadn't heard our whispered conversation. "I'm not trying to pressure you one way or another, either. If you do present a complaint, though, I'm ready to testify for you. After all, I happen to be the only witness to your kidnapping—besides Erkan, of course."

"Erkan. Oh!" Her shoulders tensed.

"Yes. I hadn't actually asked him to meet us," Dr. Neyrev said. "We ran into each other by chance in the town center this afternoon, after the smugglers dropped us off. He offered to help with our bags, which was fortunate, because I'm sure we couldn't have managed everything alone."

"Does Erkan know Sanjit's here?" Preen asked. The fear in her voice was so sharp I decided that leaving my shotgun in the car that day last April had been a mistake.

"I don't know," Dr. Neyrev said. "I didn't mention it to him. Sanjit probably doesn't care to have his smuggling activities discussed."

"You should warn Erkan about him," she said.

Dr. Neyrev looked confused. "I thought Sanjit was a friend of Erkan's."

"Maybe he was," Preen said. "Not anymore."

"Why do you care so much about Erkan?" I broke in. Her face went blank, like a curtain coming down. I couldn't blame her—coming out that way, it sounded terrible. But what I meant was, 'If you're worried that Sanjit might hurt Erkan, why can't you see he could also hurt you?'

"Dr. Neyrev, can you warn him?" she went on, like I hadn't said anything. Just as well.

"We've arranged to meet at the Holiday Home tomorrow morning, so I'll let him know then that Sanjit's likely to be frequenting Duna."

"What is Erkan helping you with?" Preen asked.

"We've been working together to compile information about missing people—especially Rayad fighters," Dr. Neyrev said. "If nothing else, we hope to be able to let families know where their loved ones are buried."

Preen's face softened into an expression I hadn't seen on it often. Almost like hope. "I wonder..." She caught my eye and her voice trailed away.

Mrs. Neyrev patted her husband's arm. "Seeing as you told Erkan you'd meet him in the morning, why don't you get some rest?" She glanced at the clock that sat on top of the television set.

It had stopped at 11:56 about a month ago, but she wouldn't know that.

"I think we could all stand a good night's sleep," she added.

Sufya stuck her head in the doorway. "We're back," she called, in her thick Sevian accent. "Did Lashmi sleep the whole time?"

"I never heard a sound from her," Arjun said.

When he got up and went over to his wife, she kissed him on the mouth in front of everybody. He turned red all the way to his ears. Sufya laughed.

For a minute, I let my mind drift to what Preen might do if I kissed her. What I'd do if she kissed me back. All the ways we could have spent a much better evening...

While I was daydreaming, Preen slipped away. I followed and caught her as she was going through the old velvet curtain that hung in the doorframe of her mother's bedroom. "Wait a minute, Preen. Explain something to me. You say we should let Sanjit be, but at the same time you're terrified he'll go after your friend, Erkan."

She fiddled with the fringe on the edge of the curtain. "You don't understand."

"Maybe not. You could help me." I took her wrist and turned her around to face me. "Do you love Erkan?"

She got still—as still as a deer just before it bolts. "My head hurts and I'm going to bed. Besides we can't talk here. We'll wake up Sitabi."

"Just answer my question, please."

"I don't know."

"That's no answer."

"Well, I don't know," she repeated, louder. "All I know is, Erkan and me, we both survived the war. We both understand what it's like to be a prisoner. We both understand what it's like to lose somebody you love."

"In other words, you're broken in the same places."

The muscles in her thin wrists tensed to pull away from me, but she didn't move.

"That doesn't mean you'll make a good fit." I looked into her eyes, but they were still blank. Maybe it wasn't that she didn't want to let me in—maybe she couldn't.

"Kiva, I'm going to marry you! Why do you have to act so jealous?"

"You're only going through with this whole thing for Sitabi, aren't you?"

"What thing?"

"Marrying me. You know I'll take care of you and be a good father for Sitabi." I took a long breath. "Whether you love me or not, you'll cook my meals and sleep with me and be Mrs. Kiva Manjali the rest of your life, because it's what our families want. Isn't that true?"

"I picked what I wanted the first time. You know how that turned out."

"Can we tell each other the truth for once? You don't love me. Just say it."

"I want to love you," she whispered. "But I don't deserve you."

"Don't deserve me?" That came so unexpected I almost laughed. Good thing I caught myself in time—it wasn't funny. "What do you mean?"

She bowed her head. "You're good. I'm not."

"Of course you're good. God made you good."

"But then I went and ruined it."

"Rama's been laid to rest, and now here's your chance to start over—with me."

She didn't answer. I gave her a little shake. "Right?"

She looked up and past me, chewing her bottom lip. "Did you hear what Dr. Neyrev said about the missing fighters?"

"Mama?" Sitabi called in her croaky night voice. "Mama, where are you? I'm thirsty."

Preen tugged her hands free. "See, I told you we'd wake up Sitabi."

"Preen, wait! All that talk earlier, that wasn't really about Sanjit, was it? That was about you. You don't want us to do anything to him because you don't think you're worth defending. You don't believe you deserve justice—or love—or anything good. Just because you didn't fancy the fellow your parents had picked for you, and decided to pick your own."

"Mama..." Sitabi whined from the bedroom.

I lifted Preen's chin so she had to look me in the eyes. "I've forgiven you and so has the whole family. God's forgiven you. Why can't you believe that?"

"Sitabi needs a drink," she said.

Chapter Thirteen: Preen

Sitabi sucked her water down and handed the cup back to me.

"Goodnight, Baby Girl." I started for the door, but she popped out from under her blanket and scooted across the mattress toward me.

"I'm scared, Mommy. Don't go."

"There's nothing to be scared of here." I made a show of searching the room, looking behind the window curtain, opening the wardrobe door.

The bag of shiny green fabric lying beside it caught my eye. Was it only this afternoon Kiva and I had fought about the color? Maybe it didn't matter much if my wedding dress was green for a virgin or white for a widow. But if Kiva and I were going to spend the rest of our lives together, I hoped it wasn't just his memories of me he was in love with.

Mother's voice came from the hall, asking a question, and Kiva answered. Something about 'getting it tomorrow.'

It sounded like he was leaving. His foot hit a loose board by the woodbox and it squeaked like a rat in a feed sack.

"What's that noise?" Sitabi whimpered. "I'm scared."

"If you go to sleep, God will send angels with good dreams."

She popped her thumb in her mouth and curled up again. Her eyes never left my face.

"The night is for sleep, so you need to sleep."

"I never sleep at night," she said, without taking out her thumb.

"Oh no?"

"Never."

"Well, little owl, you need to sleep now."

"Don't go, please." She sat up again.

"I'll stay for five more minutes, all right?" I sat down beside her on the mattress and pulled the blanket up to her chin. As her breathing slowed, so did mine. Her curls made the softest, most perfect circles around her head.

"Will that man come?" Sitabi's eyes were as dark and wide as a baby deer's.

My heart dropped. Not much got past her. "What man?"

"The scary man on the horse."

"No." I clenched my fists, making it a promise.

"Not here?"

"Never here."

"Why not?"

"Because he won't. Now go to sleep."

"I'm not sleepy."

"You have to try."

Why did everybody have to pay for my mistakes? Even my baby girl wasn't free.

I traced the design on her woven blanket—Three Peaks—the weaving pattern Mother taught me when I was just a few years older than Sitabi. The black and red pattern wobbled and blurred before my eyes. Rama and I had shared a blanket with the same pattern in Dor through many chilly nights.

Where was he lying now?

Dr. Neyrev's accented voice sounded in my head. 'If nothing else, we hope to be able to let families know where their loved ones are buried.'

If he knew where Rama had been taken after we left his body in the alley, he would have told me. But maybe Erkan had found out later, when things calmed down. Or maybe he knew somebody who knew. I could ask him—but what would Kiva say?

"If my real daddy was here, he would hit that man and make him run," Sitabi said. "He'd scare him so bad."

"You mean Rama?"

"Yes. He'd make the horse buck, and that bad man would fall off and die."

My throat squeezed up so tight it got hard to breathe. Too bad Rama couldn't hear her. That would have made him smile.

"When my real daddy gets back from dead, he's going to get that bad man. And his horse."

"That man's not coming back here. I promised, remember?"

"Mmmm."

"Now, lie quiet and I'll sing you the angel song."

Sitabi's thumb slipped toward the corner of her mouth. Her eyelids drooped. Dark eyelashes brushed her cheek.

I sat with her for a long time, stroking her hair, looking her over for hints of me that I might have missed before. No question about it, she was her daddy's girl. It hurt my heart to think she'd never know him—because of me.

***

Thursday afternoon, our first winter butchering, I caught Kiva at the door before he headed into the tub room to wash up. He'd done the work of two all day, and looked it. Flecks of blood spattered every inch of him the butcher's apron hadn't covered. Fresh blisters from the bone saw swelled between the calluses on his hands. A rip in his jeans showed a matching scrape down his shinbone.

The freezer truck from Duna Market had driven up half an hour ago, but I hadn't expected them to be done with the loading until after dark.

"Three down, three to go," he said. "But the rain's coming in, so we decided to call it a day."

"Kiva." I took a deep breath to calm the jitters in my stomach. "I need you to do something big for me. For me and Sitabi both."

"Tonight?"

"No. When you have time."

The mud caked on his boots crumbled to the floor as he jerked the laces open. "Say the word and consider it done." He rubbed a sleeve across his weary face and smiled up at me.

"Help me find out where Rama's buried."

If I knew for certain Rama had a place to lie—hadn't just been thrown away like trash—maybe I'd be able to tell Kiva what he had a right to know before I became his wife. 'Rayad fighters took your husband's body,' Sanjit had told me. 'They honored him with a funeral and a grave.'

I hadn't believed him, but what if he'd been telling the truth for once?

Kiva stared at me.

"I want you take me to Duna tomorrow to see Erkan," I said.

Kiva's eyebrows drew together. "Why?"

"He might know where Rama is buried." Kiva shook his head, puzzled.

"I don't see what Erkan has to do with it."

"Didn't you hear what Dr. Neyrev said? They've been working to get the missing fighters identified. Tracking down relatives and friends. Finding grave-sites." I swallowed to get the rasp out of my voice. "I want to know where Rama's is—if I can."

He leaned his broad shoulders back against the wall and blew out his breath so it lifted a loose twist of hair on his forehead.

I waited, standing still but with my heart galloping. Trying to fit the mismatched pieces of my life together—past and future—hill farm and ruined city—Kiva and Rama—made me wonder if even God could fix the mess I'd made.

Kiva groaned. "It's over. He's gone. Why do you have to keep going back there?"

"I don't know."

"When I look back at our life together, all the way from when we were kids, I don't see nothing but years and years of happy days,"

Kiva said softly. "New calves in the spring, fresh meat in the fall. You sneaking away from your loom to follow me and Arjun when we checked the hill pastures. Weren't you happy?"

"Mostly."

"You seemed like a girl who'd hardly have a sorrow her whole life long."

I shook my head. If that's how he saw me, no wonder he was confused. He was a man—he'd never understand what it was like to grow up knowing exactly how many cows you were worth. He'd never been scared he might end up sold to someone awful.

"But then you ran off with Rama and he brought you nothing but shame and sadness and almost got you killed."

"He loved me," I said. He loved me, but I killed him, I tried to say, but my mouth wouldn't form the words.

Kiva set his boots side by side underneath the bench beside the red rubber boots I used when it was muddy. He moved mine so all the toes would all be even. "I love you more," he said, very low. "Not that you care."

If only I could take the truth that hurt too much to speak aloud and plant it in Kiva's brain. "When there was fighting in our neighborhood, I wasn't hardly ever scared if Rama was around," I said. "Having him was like having a wolf to guard me. Didn't matter who might be in the street, or outside the door. He was so brave, he made me brave." Some nights he'd stand for hours, staring into the dark outside our apartment window. His slender body looked as much a weapon as the rifle he held.

"Maybe Rama wasn't a good man," I said. "But he would have bled every drop for Sitabi and me. If you can't honor him for that, then..."

Kiva sat so still a fly landed and crawled around on the back of his hand. He didn't swat it away, just stared at me, a long, deep stare that made me wonder if he could see in my face what I didn't dare say. His eyes got wet around the corners.

"That's how I feel, anyway," I whispered. For a little while, Rama had been my adventure. My fighter. My taste of freedom.

A long time later—it felt like an hour—Kiva finally moved. Leaning forward, he caught both my hands and pressed them between his grimy ones. He kissed the tips of my fingers. "I'm going to take care of you better than Rama ever did."

Chapter Fourteen: Kiva

Preen stood in front of me, chewing her lip, like she wanted to say something more but didn't know how. "Could we go to Dovni tomorrow? You won't be able to butcher because the weather's supposed to be bad— rain."

"Yes," I said slowly. "But—"

Tomorrow we were headed to Moltoy to buy Arjun's bull. Our bull. Monster, I'd named him in my head. How could she have forgotten the plan so soon?

"You're not going to butcher in the rain, are you?"

"No." I stopped, hoping that something would jog her memory. No way could I tell her, 'I've got a stud bull to collect for your bride price tomorrow. Finding your husband's grave can wait.'

"If I can know where he lies, I need to know." Her voice caught like she was trying not to cry.

Sufya hurried past, headed for the tub room, with a kettle of boiling water in each hand.

"You'd better wash up before you go home, or you'll make your truck smell awful," Preen said.

I pulled my filthy shirt away from my body and looked at it. Some blood had trickled down inside my right glove and stained the shirtsleeve in a ring around my wrist.

She tapped the back of my hand. "Let me take that shirt. It'll need to soak. The jeans, too. You can borrow some of Father's old clothes."

I was the one who'd spent the last hour loading meat into the freezer truck in the wind and rain, but it was her fingers that were ice-cold. Shucking off my shirt and jeans, I went to the kitchen in my long underwear to get a cup of tea while Sufya got the bath ready.

Preen followed and sat down at the table. I filled cups for both of us from the samovar.

A fly buzzed around the lampshade. The first freeze a few days ago had killed off most of them—one of the reasons we waited to butcher until the weather was really cold—but a few stragglers always lasted another week or so in the house.

She swatted at it, then sighed and slumped down against the wickerwork chair back. Suddenly I had an idea. "Why don't you call Erkan tonight and ask him what he knows about a grave, or—" Maybe he wouldn't know anything, and we could drive down to Moltoy tomorrow after all.

Sooner or later, Preen would have to remember she'd said she'd come. I should have told Sitabi we were going on a road trip to buy a bull. She wouldn't have let either of us forget it for a minute.

Preen narrowed her eyes at me. "Did I hear you right? You want me to call Erkan?"

"You said you thought he could help you."

"Well, I can't. For one thing, he gave me his phone when he rescued me from Sanjit, and I never gave it back." Preen folded her arms across her chest. "For another, even if he's got a new phone by now, if you found out I had his number, you'd be mad."

My face heated up. I hadn't been fair to him that day. What possessed me to offer him money like he'd brought back a straying cow, I'd never know. Besides, I couldn't blame him for not being able to take his eyes off Preen. Even though she'd shaved her head in the spring, and gotten thin as skim milk, she was still the prettiest girl in Tur Kej.

"So will you go with me to Duna? Sufya should be able to look after Sitabi for a few hours while we're gone."

Seemed pointless to go out fox-chasing in hopes we'd find someone who might know where Rama lay—if he even has a grave. But for some reason, it was important to Preen. Maybe Arjun could drive down and pick up Monster. Or I could ask my mother to spare one of the fellows from her store. I sighed. "Sure."

She didn't smile, but her hazel eyes got so warm they almost glowed.

The front door crashed open, making us both jump. Arjun came in, dripping, with sleet sparkling on his shoulders and woolen hat.

"Getting worse out there?" I asked.

Arjun groaned. "You're not washed up yet? I thought I gave you plenty of time."

I waved him by. "Sorry, man—I got talking. You go first."

He turned and went back down the hall to the tub room.

Preen and I were alone again with all the things we weren't saying.

She hadn't touched the tea I poured for her. "It's like a chain," Preen said softly, tracing a pattern of links on the tablecloth with one finger.

I had no idea what she was talking about, so I took Dr. Neyrev's advice, kept quiet, and listened.

"Desh—Erkan's brother—helped Rama when he first came to Dor. Rama kept Maxim from shooting Erkan. Erkan helped me escape from Sanjit in Camp Peace."

I nodded, and focused on scraping flecks of dried blood off my fingernails. She'd talk more if I wasn't looking at her.

"But it goes the other way, too. Sanjit only kidnapped me because he couldn't hurt Rama anymore. And he wouldn't have been chasing Rama in the first place if Rama hadn't told Maxim Porofky which houses had weapons stockpiled in them. And the only reason Rama did that was to save Erkan—because he was Desh's brother."

I kept quiet because I didn't know what to say. With all the good things we had ahead of us, why did she have to keep looking back? Our rooms at my family house in Duna were almost ready, painted bright yellow just like she asked. Next year's calves would be the strongest yet. Arjun and I might be able to start trading farther afield, in Moltoy or even Klim. Sitabi was growing so fast—she needed a whole family and a mama with light instead of darkness in her eyes.

"Rama gave the White Horses the information they wanted, so they let Erkan live," Preen said. "Erkan and Rama both. They were released after the IPF came. Or maybe right before. But that didn't help Rama any. He'd given away Rayad secrets, so Rais Sundar sent Sanjit after him."

Her freckled nose and soft voice didn't match the terrible doings she talked of. It made me sick to listen—to think what Rama had dragged her through. Respect him I could not, but for Preen's sake, I'd try to understand. Maybe when we found his grave, she'd be able to say goodbye once and for all.

Preen rubbed her eyes. "Rama said he'd kill Maxim or die trying, and I couldn't talk sense into him." She stopped. Most girls would have cried some, or at least sniffled, but Preen just sat there, staring wide-eyed at our tea glasses on the tabletop.

Arjun came out of the tub room in his boxer shorts and tee shirt, rubbing the twists of hair on his head with a towel. "Your turn, Kiva," he called. "The water's still warm."

Preen gasped like she'd been startled awake and made a sour face at her brother. "No, he'll need fresh." She turned to me. "I'll boil you another kettle."

She got up and hoisted one of the big, rusty bath kettles into the sink and turned on the tap. Water rushed in to fill it.

Preen, there's something you aren't telling me, I thought. *Something I should probably know.*

***

Friday started out windy, spitting rain, with sunshine here and there between the clouds. Thankfully, it wasn't near as cold as predicted. First thing in the morning, I drove up to the Rastikar farm and went to the barn to find Arjun.

He was in the dairy room getting the milk ready for pickup. The smell of the bleach he used to clean the place curled the hairs inside my nose. Like always, he'd used too much.

A row of empty two-liter glass bottles stood on a table by the shiny metal milk tank. One by one, he filled them from the spigot on the tank.

"Got a favor to ask," I said.

"Sure." He twisted the spigot closed just in time to stop the bottle overflowing. A few white bubbles escaped down the side.

"I know the plan was for me to go get that bull today, but I promised Preen—"

"Isn't she coming with you?"

"Well, the plan changed. We're not going to Moltoy. We're going to Duna to see if we can find out anything about where Rama's buried—or if he's buried. I think Dr. Neyrev talking about his project with the refugees put the idea in her head."

Arjun set the bottle on the milk table. He wiped it clean and screwed the cap on. He didn't look at me but I knew by the set of his head he was listening. "Any reason you can't go to find out more about Rama another day?"

"No."

"So why don't you?"

"If you'd seen the look in her eyes when she asked me..."

Arjun nodded.

"I couldn't tell her no." I shrugged. "Besides, I'm about out of ideas. I do everything right, and she takes it all wrong. Just can't win with her."

"Mmmm," said Arjun. He turned the spigot on the dairy tank and a white stream gushed into another bottle.

"She can't think of nothing but that dead Rama of hers." I stared down at the bleach-water puddled on the cement floor, choking back weeks of anger and disappointment.

Arjun straightened and rubbed his hands on his shirt, brushing one sleeve across his forehead to push away the little twists of hair. "You jumped in front of Sanjit's gun to protect her not so long ago."

"That was easy. This is—"

He crossed the room and put an arm around my shoulders in that annoying big-brother way he had. For once it felt good. I didn't step away. "You've been honest with me, so I'll be honest with you," he said. "I'm worried for my sister. If you decide to break the engagement, I doubt she'll ever get another husband. She'll spend her life alone."

"What about Erkan?" It came out sounding as bitter as I felt.

Arjun gave me a look.

"It's just—this is not what I signed up for." My voice echoed through the big room.

"I'm not sure anybody who gets married gets what he signed up for."

"You can't talk—Sufya's crazy about you."

"Sufya's family disowned her when she married me," he said. "They haven't spoken a word to her since. Not even her mother."

"Didn't know that."

He unbuttoned his shirt and pulled his undershirt down to show me a pattern of splashy red scars across his chest.

"That happened in Dor?"

"Some people didn't take kindly to a dirty Tur marrying a Sevian girl."

"Acid?"

He nodded. "At the bus stop one night. Preen doesn't know about it. Don't tell her."

I sighed. The heat in my stomach had begun to cool. "But Sufya loves you," I said, cringing inside at how whiny it sounded.

"Kiva, Preen loves you, too. If I wasn't sure of that, I wouldn't have said anything about—anything."

The rumble of a diesel engine outside told me the milk truck had arrived.

Arjun hurried over to the stack of plastic crates in the corner and started filling them with bottles.

I stayed where I was, hands limp at my sides and heart as heavy as a stone. "I'm taking her to Duna because I have no idea what else to do. But can you drive down to Moltoy for me and pick up that bull? I'll text you all the information."

Arjun hoisted a milk crate to his shoulder and smiled. "Should be able to. And Kiva—I think God's got it figured out."

"Can you pray for me? For the both of us? Seems like God listens to you."

"Oh, I do. Every day."

Chapter Fifteen: Kiva

Preen and I took my car to Duna and left the truck with Arjun.

I didn't tell Preen how she'd changed our plan. The more I thought about it, the more I realized it didn't matter much. Arjun could bring the bull home as easy as I could, though I felt bad asking him to go collect his own gift.

On the drive down, we didn't talk. I drove. She stared out the window at the heavy gray clouds and the hills going by, her stubborn little chin in her hand.

Preen had said Erkan was staying at the Holiday Home, so that's where we went. Since it was Duna's only real hotel, it was crammed with refugees from Dor Province who didn't have family in Tur Kej. How long they would stay, or where they hoped to go afterwards, was anybody's guess.

We didn't have to go inside the hotel to find Erkan. He'd set up shop under the veranda at the front, with his tattooing kit laid out beside him on a pillowcase. His client sat on the tiled veranda floor, using his other arm to brace himself against a stone vase filled with wilted orange flowers.

Erkan dug a tiny needle brush into the man's shoulder with quick, precise strokes, creating a curved line. He was so focused on the design forming under his hands that we probably could have stood there watching him all day, if the man he was tattooing hadn't jerked his head toward us and said something in Sev. Strange for me to hear Tur people talking Sev, but Preen must have been used to it.

Erkan looked up.

Preen took a long breath and tucked her hands into the sleeves of her sweater.

"That's some good work," I said, coming closer. "Some of the best I've ever seen."

"Should be. I'm a Durband." Erkan dabbed a trickle of ink and blood away. "I know every design we Tur ever invented—plus a few. They're all in my head."

True or not, his work was worth a second look. A fresh pattern of interlocked circles ran across the arm above the line of diamonds that marked the man as a Martaza—one of the few Tur families that stayed in Dor city after the war in the 50's.

I pulled up a sleeve and examined my own ink. Some of it was sloppy and most of it had faded over the years—the left arm had never even been finished.

Erkan raised his eyebrows. "Who in the world did you?"

"Some old fellow my cousin's husband hired."

When Arjun's father had taken him to be tattooed the year he became a man, my mother sent me along, even though I wasn't but fifteen. Better early then never, she'd decided, since my father wasn't living.

Erkan took my hand and held it palm-up in his. He rolled back my sleeve to the elbow and shook his head. "He might have been good—a long time ago."

"Before his eyesight went and he started drinking," Preen said.

I looked down at her in surprise. "You remember all that?"

She made a scornful noise. "Of course I remember the fuss your mother made. I was almost eight."

I turned back to Erkan. "Maybe you could touch me up someday."

"Maybe I could." Erkan smiled, all on one side. The burn scars seemed to have frozen the right side of his face. "I owe you at least twenty dinars worth of work."

Hopefully he'd forgiven me for the other day.

"That's enough for now," Erkan told his client.

The man nodded.

Erkan smeared some kind of antiseptic cream over the fresh, raw design and wrapped the arm in gauze. Each movement was slow and careful, like he had all the time in the world.

The man stood and stretched out his bandaged arm, sucking a painful breath through his teeth. "I'll be back in a week for the rest."

Erkan nodded. "Sounds good."

The man headed back inside Holiday Home. The double doors swung closed behind him, creaking on tight hinges.

Preen knelt down beside Erkan on the tiles. "Do you know what happened to Rama's body? Nobody's ever told me where he was taken or if he got buried." Once she started, her words came spilling out in a rush. "If you know, or if you heard anything, please tell me."

Erkan stuck the needle brush in a bottle of rubbing alcohol and cleaned his hands with a wipe. "If I knew," he said slowly. "I would have already told you. But I don't. Sorry."

Preen's shoulders drooped. "You never heard nothing?" she whispered.

"No. There are so many missing people, Preen. So many."

She got to her feet, pulling her baggy sweater close around her. "I was sure you'd know, since you're helping Dr. Neyrev."

"No. But I do know who you could ask—Padmi Farhanji. Padmi knows everything about everybody."

"Who's she?" I asked.

"A lot of things," Erkan said. "Most importantly, the Rais of Dor, ever since Sundar Farhanji was killed. She and Desh worked together a lot back in the Rayad days. That's how I know her." He slipped his mobile phone out of his jacket. "I'm also friends with one of her bodyguards. Let me give Semyon a call—he'll get you in to see her. Personal favor."

Semyon didn't answer his phone, so Erkan said he'd come with us to talk to Rais Padmi at the Tur Kej Rais's residence.

As we walked back to the car, Erkan's eyes followed Preen like a thirsty man looks at a glass of cold water. As for me, except for the ink on my arms, I might as well have been invisible.

Preen sidled close to me and slipped her hand into mine. I squeezed her fingers.

What's the point of trying to find Rama's grave? I wanted to ask her. What difference will it make? But I didn't know a way to say it that didn't sound bad.

***

When we got out of the car, Erkan led the way to the main gate. I'd passed the whitewashed stone walls of our Rais's compound dozens of times, but I'd only gone inside once before—for the funeral of Amin Rastikar, Preen's father. He'd been one of Rais Manjal's councilors.

"You do realize that Rais Manjal's visiting schedule is full for the next three weeks?" the guard at the gate asked, never taking his eyes off his phone. "Still, I can put your names down, and if there's an opening—"

"We're here for Rais Padmi," Erkan said.

"Oh." The guard raised his eyebrows. "All right, then." He grabbed a radio from the table beside it. "Semyon Deshi, over to Gate One."

The response was a burst of static. The heavy steel gate slid open and the guard waved the three of us inside. We walked into a small cement room where two more guards waited.

Before they patted us down, Erkan tossed an ivory-handled switchblade and the leather case that held his needle kit into a basket on the guards' desk.

When they were done, they dragged open another gate, and we stepped through into the sunshine.

Rais Manjal's residence and the Council Buildings made a half-circle inside the walls. The black flags of the Tur Raises flapped at each corner of the compound. Smaller Sevian flags flew beneath them—white, with the three red stars.

The buildings were all long, low, whitewashed concrete except for one stone tower—older than everything else in the place put together, by the look of it.

I remembered all that from my last visit. What I hadn't expected was how crowded the place would be. Looked like anyone from Dor who could claim the name Farhanji had showed up for a big family reunion.

They'd pitched tents all over the Rais's lawn, parked motorbikes against the wall, strung lines of washing between trees where the members of the Tur Kej Council used to sit in the shade and drink tea. A dog barked from inside one of the council buildings. A couple of children chased a football down the wide gravel walk. Two women with their heads wrapped in flowered kerchiefs like Sevians sat on the marble lip of a huge ornamental fountain and smoked.

"Semyon should be here already," Erkan muttered, looking around.

A man with a rifle slung across his back jogged toward us.

Erkan met him halfway and thumped his chest with a clenched fist. "Semyon! What's going on, man? I've been calling you and calling you."

"Sorry," Semyon said. "I dropped my phone in the water the other day and the battery's no good anymore." He tipped his chin toward the huge ornamental fountain in the center of the Rais's lawn. Twists of dirty hair hung loose to his shoulders, but they didn't do much to hide his slashed-off ear or the scar that ran from jaw to collarbone. His accent told me he wasn't from Dor—before the war chewed him up and spat him out, he'd most likely been a farmer somewhere in our hills, like me. Like Rama.

Semyon took us to meet Padmi Farhanji, the Rais of Dor, in the council building on the left-hand side of the compound. Now that Simon Nevin was president, the Rais of Dor was really Rais of nowhere. But Padmi kept busy, Semyon told us, pestering countries that weren't part of the European League to accept refugees from Sevia. She was even trying to get them to take former Rayad members.

Rais Padmi looked younger than I expected—not more than fifty, for sure. She had at least ten piercings in each ear, and her iron-gray hair was even shorter than Preen's. She sat at one end of a big leather couch with her feet tucked up under her. A tablet computer lay on the low table beside her.

As we walked in, a big gray dog got slowly to its feet, a growl rising in its throat.

"Easy, Wolf," Rais Padmi called. "They're with Semyon."

The dog settled itself back on the rug. I could have sworn it smiled at Rais Padmi, ears pricked forward to catch her words. Its tail swished across the rug.

"Come in," she said to us. "Don't worry about Wolf. He's one of the good ones."

We walked toward her across a red rug so thick it squished like moss under our shoes.

"I'm Kiva Manjali. And this is Preen—Enda." I almost slipped up and said Rastikar. "My fiancee."

"But you're not from Dor, are you?" Rais Padmi asked. "Rais Manjal is the one to talk to if there's a problem about the marriage."

"No, there's no problem." At least none she could help us with. "We've got our papers ready. And a date."

"Congratulations. So what did you come to see me for?"

Preen ran her tongue across her lower lip. "I'm looking for—" she swallowed. "My husband's grave."

"I see," Rais Padmi said softly. "Tell me about him."

"His name was Rama Enda. He had the Enda tattoos on both arms. Rayad horns on his right wrist and bull-rider's bands on his left." Preen pressed the sleeve of her thick sweater to her nose.

I put a hand on her back. She was trembling, but her voice came steady.

Rais Padmi nodded. She picked up her tablet and tapped the screen. "Let me record that."

"He died on April fifth of this year."

"Where?"

"In Dor—the city."

"Do you know a more specific location?"

Preen took a long breath. "It happened in front of Porofky's, this little grocery store on Bladik Street. Sevian side of the line."

"How did he die?" Rais Padmi asked.

Preen's face lost all color. Her eyes caught mine, then flashed away. She gasped for air like she'd been running.

We all waited for her to keep talking, but she didn't.

"Do you know?"

Preen covered her face with both hands so I could barely hear what she whispered. "I killed him. He threw a grenade at me, and I threw it back."

The floor of the Council House tipped sideways under my feet. Everything got blurry the way it does sometimes when you stand up too fast. My eyes burned, my throat burned, and I had to keep swallowing the yell that wanted to break out—Oh, Preen, why didn't you ever tell me? Why did you think you had to bear that alone?

I started toward her.

She backed away.

"Come here," I said.

She shook her head, eyes and mouth wide. "I didn't mean to do it," she gasped. "It just—happened. It was—I don't—" Her words came in ragged gasps. "I don't even know how—"

I wrapped my arms around her from behind, holding her against me as tight and warm as I knew how to do.

She still shook. Her fingers dug into my arm so hard I'd probably find marks later.

For a long minute, the only sounds in the room were Wolf's tail thumping the rug and Preen's loud, scared breathing.

Rais Padmi scrolled through a list of names on her tablet.

Erkan paced back and forth, his arms locked across his chest.

Semyon stared at the ceiling and twirled a lock of his hair around his finger.

"So could you give us an idea where Rama might lie?" I asked, to break the horrible silence. My voice sounded way too normal.

"I wish I could help you more," Rais Padmi said, "But we're very busy here, as I'm sure you know. Let me make a few phone calls over the weekend." She gave Preen an encouraging smile. "Mrs. Enda, as soon as I know anything, I'll have Erkan contact you."

"Let me go." Preen pushed against my arms. "I'm all right."

I didn't want to, but I let her slip free. Preen handed Erkan her phone and he punched in his number. She watched him, chewing her bottom lip. It brought a little color back to her face, but not much.

"I was there when Rama died," Erkan said, looking at me instead of Rais Padmi. "Saw the whole thing. Preen isn't to blame. If she hadn't had the sense to toss that grenade back out the shop window, both she and the Sevian woman with her might have been killed instead."

He handed the phone back to Preen. Faint, rusty spots covered both sleeves of his yellow jacket. Bloodstains. I hadn't noticed them before.

My heart hurt so bad I couldn't breathe. No wonder Preen felt safer with Erkan than with me. He knew how Rama had died. He'd witnessed the worst moment of her life. No ugly secrets between them. But now I knew, too, so maybe—

Rais Padmi broke into my thoughts. "Mrs. Enda, if your husband's grave exists, we'll find out where it is, I promise."

Preen let out her breath like she'd been holding it. "I'm sorry about your husband, too," she whispered.

"I lost him six years ago. But what does a woman my age want with long hair?" She rubbed her salt and pepper hair.

"Padmi, Dr. Neyrev's meeting me at the hotel in an hour," Erkan said. "So I'd better be going. He'll come back here with me after lunch."

"Good," Rais Padmi said.

Erkan turned to leave the Council Chamber, but Preen reached out and caught the sleeve of his jacket.

"Wait. I meant to tell you—Sanjit's in Duna."

Erkan stopped. "Is he? Somehow, I'm not surprised." He sighed. "Takes all kinds..."

Rais Padmi sat up straighter on her couch. "Do you mean Sanjit Sind, the pimp from Tur Fen?"

"Yes, him." Preen rubbed the sleeve of her sweater across her face.

"So Sanjit Sind made it out of Dor after all," Rais Padmi said, like she was talking to herself. "Why are people like that always the survivors?"

"He told me he's done selling girls," Preen said. "He's going to inherit the farm south of ours from his uncle."

"Is he, now?" Rais Padmi's voice carried an edge that could cut. "How lucky."

Erkan muttered something in Sev.

"Exactly," Rais Padmi said. "A traitor. He gave Rayad a bad name and took advantage of our Tur people during their darkest time. Shame on him for making money off women who had nowhere else to turn." Her head snapped up. "Where did you say he's staying?"

With her dark eyes locked on mine, I'd never been so glad I had nothing to hide.

"I think he's at his uncle Manish's farm, waiting for the man to die so he can take it over. But we're considering bringing a complaint to—"

She ignored me and flicked her finger across the tablet screen. "I'm going to add Sanjit to my elimination list for next week. There are a few besides him still running around who should have been dealt with before now." She glanced up and down the screen. "Things get so disorganized during an evacuation."

A cold shock ran down my back as I realized what she'd said. "Wait a minute! You're going to kill him?"

"Don't worry about Sanjit. A bullet in the head is a blessing compared to what he put some of my young Rayad women through." Rais Padmi pressed her mouth into a grim line.

"Sounds like the Sanjit problem will be solved without us lifting a finger." Erkan said, glancing at Preen.

Rais Padmi nodded. "Yes, but I thought you'd want to—"

He waved a hand quickly. "Oh, no, not me."

"Fine. Ashuk and Semyon work well together on these jobs." She tapped the screen of her tablet again. "Many of our fighters were buried around Klim," Rais Padmi added after a moment, looking up at Preen again. "But we tried to bring the ones from the Tur provinces back up into the hills if we could. So there are some graves around Moltoy, too. It's possible your husband is there."

Preen's eyes went wide. "Moltoy? Oh, Kiva, the bull!"

Chapter Sixteen: Preen

I clapped a hand over my mouth. How could I have forgotten Friday was the day of our trip to Moltoy? Buying that bull—Monster—meant the beginning of the best, strongest herd we'd ever had. Not to mention it was the better part of my bride price.

Rais Padmi gave me a puzzled glance and went back to fiddling with her tablet.

"I'm sorry, Kiva," I whispered. "Don't know how I forgot."

"Don't worry." His steady green eyes smiled down at me. "You've had a lot on your mind."

"I'm sorry about the bull. And about—" Keeping such a secret from you, I tried to add, but my voice died.

He had to be thinking twice about that New Year's wedding he'd been so set on, now that he knew—what he knew. If people could melt away for shame, I'd be a wet spot on the rug. I searched his face for shock, or anger, or horror, but saw only sadness crinkling up his eyes.

Kiva ran a hand over my head, smoothing my hair down, tucking the rough bits behind my ears. "Forget about it. Arjun's going to get Monster. Bringing you here was more important. Much more. I see that now. I'm not mad, but I wish—I wish you hadn't been scared to tell me."

I nodded, swallowing tears. Now that the truth about Rama's death wasn't a secret anymore, the horror of what I'd done dwindled to a quiet sadness. Out in the open, no shame was as awful as it appeared when hidden in the dark.

"If I'd known why you kept pushing me away every time I tried to get close, then—"

"I thought if you knew, you'd leave me. Then Sitabi wouldn't have a father."

The picture of my little girl's eyes shining up at Kiva while he messed with her curls flashed into my mind. He couldn't be Rama, but he was the perfect man to fill the place Rama had left. Maybe he'd even fill it better than Rama could have.

"Sitabi needs you," I said.

His breath hitched. "I know that. But what about you?"

"I'm so sorry." All the things I wanted to say, but couldn't, came welling up and shriveled away to nothing on my tongue. Someday I should write them all down and give him the paper. I'd never thought of that before. Just because I couldn't talk right didn't mean I couldn't share my thoughts.

I closed my eyes and hot tears squeezed out the corners. "Why should you want to marry me? I'm a killer."

He took my hand and held it to his chest. His heart beat slow and steady under my fingers. "You feel that? That's my heart saying, 'I love Preenalaya. No matter what.' But I want you to need me, too."

I looked up into his serious eyes. "I do need you. Didn't you know that?"

He smiled. "Yes. But I've been waiting a long time for you to admit it."

Rais Padmi sank back into the leather couch cushions and nodded at Semyon. Our time was up.

"Take them out, and have Seeli bring me tea before the group from Klim gets here," she said.

"Come on." Semyon hitched his rifle over his shoulder and waved us ahead of him. The rifle scope clanked against something metal tucked into his belt as he walked.

We crossed the thick velvety carpet, passed Rais Padmi's big wolf-dog chained to a ring in the wall, and out through the Council House door.

The clouds had rolled back and hung in wet clumps over the hills. The patches of sky above us looked hopeful. I stared up at them and let the bright hope fill me.

Semyon looked up, too. "It's good to be home," he said. "This air—you could live a hundred years breathing this air."

"So, Semyon," Kiva's voice wavered. "When Rais Padmi tells you to kill somebody...?"

"I kill him," Semyon said.

***

In the car, Kiva leaned back in the driver's seat. His gingery topknot almost brushed the ceiling of the car. "So. About Sanjit. What do you think?"

The way Rais Padmi had condemned him to death, as casual as if she were planning her dinner, made me wish I'd kept my mouth shut. "I was just trying to warn Erkan. Didn't know Rais Padmi would have any idea who I was talking about." I folded my arms across my stomach and shivered. "It doesn't seem right. Besides, Sanjit's not even from Dor."

"Whatever happens, he won't get anything he doesn't deserve." Kiva sighed. "I think we can rest easy about that."

In my mind, I saw Sanjit riding across our pasture, moving with his horse like he'd been born on it. If God would give someone like him the chance at a new life, worrying that mine wouldn't work out was a waste of time. But maybe we'd both pay first. If you had to pay for what you did wrong, did that mean you weren't forgiven?

"I don't believe for a minute Sanjit's sorry for what he's done," Kiva said. "That kind isn't sorry until they're caught. But I don't like it either." He put the key in the ignition and started the car. "Are you cold?"

I rolled back my damp, crumpled sweater cuffs and shook my head. "I'm fine."

The tall white walls of the Rais's compound dropped behind us as we drove back toward downtown Duna. We passed the fairgrounds, a bare stretch of mud and trampled grass. The stock buildings were almost deserted, except for a few traders still waiting to close deals made at the fair last week.

Kiva's lowered eyebrows told me he was still thinking about what Rais Padmi had said. "They can't come storming up from Dor and start dispensing justice however they please like Tur Kej is the lawless wilds. Rais Padmi seems to have forgotten we have a Rais of our own. And Sanjit does, too. It's not right."

We drove by the Holiday Home, the gas station, the grocery store, the ancient oak grove in Duna Park. I sat quiet and waited. When it came to matters of justice, Kiva always had plenty to say.

"Like I've told you from the beginning, we need to bring a complaint to our Rais."

"You heard what the guard at the gate said. If we bring a complaint, Rais Manjal probably won't have time to look at it for weeks. By then it will be too late."

"That's true." He nodded, tapping his fingers on the steering wheel.

Kiva's family's department store rose from below us as we crested the hill and started down the other side. Besides the hospital, it was the biggest building in Duna. Above the automatic glass doors, a huge red and white sign read: MANJALI FASHIONS AND FABRICS.

Kiva slowed and turned off into the parking lot.

"So why bother with starting a case?" I asked. "Let's let things go as they go. If Rais Padmi's people get Sanjit he'll be just as dead as if he was executed for kidnapping. Does it matter how—"

"Yes. It matters." Kiva cut the engine and turned to face me, as serious as if he'd never smiled in his life.

"Because—"

"Because it's the difference between justice and...and..." He raked his fingers through his dreadlocks, searching for words. "You want to know why Dor burned down? It's because people don't understand the difference between doing what was right and doing what they wanted."

The tightness in my chest made it hard to breathe. "When I—when Rama died, I thought I was doing the right thing."

"Preen." He put his calloused fingers under my chin and lifted my head. "I didn't mean you. You did no wrong. You did what you had to do."

"How can you say that? You weren't there. You don't how it all happened."

"But I know you." He smiled. "That's all I need to know."

I couldn't speak. He'd heard the worst from me, and it hadn't changed his heart. He was ready to take the bitter with the sweet and keep coming back for more. Rama or no Rama, Sanjit or no Sanjit, Sitabi and I didn't have nothing to worry about.

The tightness around my heart snapped like a thread pulled too tight and I began to sob so hard my stomach hurt. Kiva hopped out of the driver's side and came around the car. He opened my door, lifted me and settled into the seat with me on his lap.

After five minutes, or ten minutes, or longer, I sat up and wiped my eyes and nose on the cuff of my sweater. Kiva's cheeks were wet too, and his eyelashes sparkled with tears.

"Why are we stopped at your family's store?" I asked.

"Because we have better things to do than talk about what happened last spring," Kiva said. "And I got the feeling you didn't love any of the fabric samples I chose the other day." He made a fake-sad face, pushing out his lower lip.

"Mmmm." I should have ignored the imagined insult to Rama and let the bag of shimmery green stuff be what Kiva meant it to be—forgiveness.

"Come on." He pushed the car door all the way open with his foot and we both climbed out. "Since we're here, how about you have a look for yourself and choose exactly the material you want for your dress."

"All right." I wiped my eyes again.

Sunshine broke through a gap in the clouds and shone on the huge red letters of the name that would soon be mine.

Kiva bowed his head and swept his arm in the direction of the store entrance. "After you. But if Mother's here we'll have to talk her out of making me stay and stock shelves for the holiday."

Kiva had worked at Manjali Fashions when he was younger, but he hated being stuck indoors. Ever since he turned eighteen he'd been at one or another of the farms that leased extra pastureland from the Manjali family. Mostly ours, because Arjun needed his help with the herd after our father died—and because I was there.

As we walked in, Kiva reached for my hand, pushed up the baggy cuff of my sweater and curled his fingers around mine. "You want a white dress, right?"

I nodded.

The first floor of Manjali Fashions had ready-made clothes—jeans, dresses, skirts, blouses, shoes. The second floor was fabrics—every kind. You name it, they had a bolt of it. That floor looked like a cross between a splintered rainbow and those scrap-patch quilts Mrs. Neyrev had in Dor. Made me dizzy.

We'd hardly been up there a minute when Sanjit Sind walked past, carrying a roll of blue fabric under his arm, the kind you'd make curtains or cushion covers with.

Fear crawled up my spine and through the roots of my hair. I moved closer to Kiva. He had his back to Sanjit, looking at a roll of white material sewn with tiny silver sequins.

Don't look up, I told Kiva in my head. Don't turn around.

Sanjit glanced up, and our eyes met. My tongue stuck to the roof of my mouth. I couldn't have said anything if I'd wanted to. Sanjit smiled, and started down the broad stairs, probably headed for the checkout counter on the first floor.

Kiva pulled the shimmery roll of fabric off the rack and shook out a length of it. "What do you think of—what's wrong?"

I took a shaky breath. "Nothing."

He frowned. "Preen..."

"Sanjit's here. He just went downstairs. He must be getting new curtains for the Sind place, or something. Seeing him so sudden gave me a turn, that's all."

Kiva tossed the fabric aside. I jumped in front of him and put both hands on his chest, shoving hard as I could to stop him heading for the stairs. He didn't notice me more than a bull would have noticed a grasshopper.

"Kiva! Stop, please!" My shrill voice echoed through the store. I grabbed his arm, lost my balance as he jerked me along, and almost fell. He turned and caught me by the elbow before I hit the slick floor. "Don't go after him," I gasped. "Leave him be."

Kiva threw up his hands in frustration. "All right, all right. But if he has any sense, he'll—"

"It's not about him," I said. "I don't want you getting hurt!" I tugged my sweater down over my hips and let my breathing slow. "He carries a gun everywhere he goes."

"So?" Kiva pushed dreadlocks out of his face and tucked them back into the knot on top of his head. "Sanjit wouldn't do nothing to me." He smiled and ran his fingertips down my cheek. "He wouldn't dare."

Chapter Seventeen: Preen

We bought three meters of the sequin fabric—and a green velour jacket with matching sweatpants, yet another pair of jeans, and fringe trim for the curtains in our new house. At the last moment, Kiva dashed back upstairs and came back panting, with a double handful of fine white netting. "For your veil," he said.

Most of the drive back to the farm, we didn't talk, but the silence between us felt cozy, like a well-worn blanket. I could look over at Kiva and smile without wondering if someday he'd turn away for good. Memories of gunfire, smoke, and my husband's blood sticky on my fingers hung farther back in my mind than they usually did.

As we passed the turn-off that led up the hill to the Sind place, Kiva slowed and looked up the gravel road, a dark scowl on his face.

"Thinking about Sanjit?" I asked.

"If I put a word in his ear about Rais Padmi's assassins, it might be the kick he needs to send him down the road back to Tur Fen," he said.

"Let me do it," I put my hand on his arm. "Sanjit knows me. We've talked before, and—"

"No!" Kiva's foot punched the gas and we shot forward. "Absolutely not."

A crow rose from a dead animal on the road ahead of us and flapped off slowly toward the hill pastures.

"Why not?" I fiddled with a loose thread in my sweater, a nervous flutter rising in my stomach. "It might be just the Sinds there—I mean Rani and Manish. Besides, Sanjit didn't try to hurt me when we met in the hill pasture."

"Honey," he said slowly, testing out the new name. "He's not going to hurt me, either. If anything, he'll thank me."

"Why?"

Kiva's forehead wrinkled in confusion. "Why not? Listen, if Sanjit loses his inheritance or his life, he's got nobody but himself to blame. I'm not going to stand by and let him be shot down in his uncle's home."

We bounced over a pothole and I squeezed his arm to steady myself.

"The shock would tip old Manish into his grave," Kiva said. "Besides, as I'm sure Arjun would remind us, the Sinds are a good family. They don't need their name dragged into a scandal."

"Rani's heart isn't too strong, either," I said. Both the Sinds had been prayer topics at Mother's last meeting.

Kiva slowed to take us around another pothole. The scrub thorns in the ditch at the edge scraped the tires of the car as we went by.

"I don't want a neighbor's death on my hands," he said. "And it's better I tell Sanjit to his face."

"Maybe."

"Well, what's the alternative? Your mother tells Rani Sind that her nephew's got a couple of killers after him at the next prayer meeting?"

Like always, Kiva knew just what to say. There was no arguing with the fellow.

"All right. I hope he listens to you. But please be careful," I said.

"Don't worry." He leaned across the gearshift and kissed the tip of my nose.

We turned up our track, rattling over the ruts the last rain had cut into the ground and pulled to a stop in the flat space beside the farmhouse.

"I'll settle all your ghosts, one by one." Kiva made a dusting-off motion with his hands and gave me that irresistible ear-to-ear grin. "Watch me."

He glanced out the car window down toward the barn. His smile vanished. "Wait a minute—there's no way Arjun could be back from Moltoy already."

I looked, too. Our livestock trailer stood on the shady side of the barn in front of the grain silo, where Kiva had parked it after the fair.

"He must not have gone. But—" Kiva cut himself off and dug his phone out of his pocket, scanning for texts or missed calls. "Don't know why he didn't call."

"So we'll find out when we go inside," I said.

***

Mother, Sitabi, Sufya, and baby Lashmi were all in the kitchen, sitting around the table. Half-empty glasses and scattered crumbs showed they must have just finished having tea.

Sufya was talking with someone on the phone.

Mother jumped up as we came in. "Dr. Neyrev's at the hospital," she said. "He collapsed right after he got up this morning."

Just like that, the happiness trickling into my heart drained away. It seemed cruel that such a trouble would strike when the Neyrevs had finally found safety.

Kiva sucked in his breath. "Is he going to be all right?"

"He looked poorly when I first saw him this morning," Mother said. "Very pale. He was coughing a lot, too." She twisted the ribbons at end of her gray braid. "He'd just walked into the kitchen when all of a sudden his eyes rolled back in his head and down he went. Thanks to God, Arjun caught him before he hit the floor, or he might have really hurt himself."

"So you won't be back tonight?" Sufya asked in Sev, holding the phone to her cheek. A worried crease formed between her eyebrows. She turned to Mother. "Arjun tell me they staying the night," she said in her baby-talk Tur.

"Ask him if they need food or anything," Mother whispered.

"Oh, right. I ask him."

Sufya lowered the phone and looked up at Kiva. "Arjun says so sorry he didn't get your bull because of hospital trip. They are at hospital now."

No surprise there. The house could be on fire, but Arjun would leave it burning and go if he thought Dr. Neyrev needed him.

Kiva's shoulders drooped. "The bull doesn't matter. I can get one next season. Arjun won't care if I'm a year late. It's a shame Dr. Neyrev should be took sick so bad. Did the doctor say what it might be?"

Mother turned to Sufya, a question in her eyes.

"I don't know the word. It's a..." Sufya tapped her chest. "They saying it's a breath problem."

"An infection in the lungs?" Mother's voice shook.

"Maybe." Sufya's eyes met mine. "So sorry for your family," she said. "It's very sad."

***

Later, Kiva sat with me on the end of Mother's bed in the room she, Sitabi and I now shared. The dull gold light of a cloudy evening made the ends of his dreadlocks glow like fire and highlighted the sturdy angles of his face.

I ran a hand over his beard, down his neck and chest. The warmth of him soaked into my fingertips and spread all through me. Happiness filled my stomach, replacing the shame that had churned inside for months.

He pulled my head down against his shoulder. "So, I was sure all was lost. That is, I was sure Monster was lost—"

"No need to get dramatic," I cut in. "You've paid more than half the bride price already."

"But I called the trader again and said we were still interested in the bull. We'd just come to get it a day or two later than we'd first planned. Tomorrow I'll drive down to Duna and trade the car for my truck, so Arjun will have a vehicle to bring the Neyrevs home when Dr. Neyrev is discharged. You and Sitabi can get ready, and we'll leave as soon as I have the trailer hooked up. Never did tell Aunt Desi we were coming, so it will be a great surprise."

"Or not." I made a face.

He threw back his head and laughed. His eyes sparkled just like Sitabi's when she was getting into mischief. No wonder they took to each other.

"Some strong Brahma blood is just what our herds need for the next few years," he added.

"If you say so."

"And you, Honey, are just what I need." He lifted the end of the shimmery white material we had bought and draped it across my head and shoulders. It almost felt like having long hair again.

"One other thing—I told Rais Padmi we had a date, but we actually don't yet, do we?"

"A date?"

"For the wedding."

I took a long breath. If Rama could see me now from wherever he was, would he be glad? He hadn't wanted my life to go on without him, but if he could have known that I'd be rescued from Sanjit and brought home to our little girl again, would he have felt different? Would he still have tossed that grenade? Maybe God would let me ask Rama someday, and maybe He wouldn't, but for now—

"What about January 3rd?" I said.

Kiva nodded. "Why not?"

"It's close enough to New Year's that the family will be gathered anyway. Hopefully Dr. Neyrev will be better by then." I tried to swallow the sadness that scraped the back of my throat. My father hadn't lived to see me married. Maybe Dr. Neyrev wouldn't, either.

"Oh, he'll be better," Kiva said. He put an arm around my shoulders and squeezed. "Dr. Neyrev is one tough old man. He's bound to be better."

"Mmmm." I couldn't feel so sure.

"A wedding on January 3rd—that sounds good," Kiva said. "The paperwork won't take a minute. We can do it a few days before. We'll go to the Council House for our witnesses' signatures, and Arjun's of course. Then there's nothing left but the party!"

Chapter Eighteen: Preen

After Kiva left to get his truck, I packed a backpack for me and Sitabi with toys, snacks, and changes of clothes for the both of us. She'd learned to go on the toilet the summer before, but just in case, I stuffed in a pair of those plastic pants she used to wear.

Erkan called while Sufya, Sitabi and I were having breakfast. Mother had finished hers and headed out to the barn for the morning milking. Since Sufya was still busy trying to get Lashmi to eat a few spoonfuls of oatmeal, I ducked out the back door.

A couple of young roosters scattered before me and ran up the sunny hillside. Their emerald-green tail feathers fluttered in the wind. I sat down on a big stone a ways up the slope because we sometimes got a better signal up there.

"It's good to hear your voice, Preen. Very good," Erkan said. His words came thick and slow like cold honey.

My heart began to race. "Did you learn anything about—"

"Last night I talked to somebody who talked to somebody who talked to somebody. But I'll spare you the details. The short story is, I found one of the guys—" the faint huff of him blowing smoke out his nose filled the pause. "One of the guys who helped to bury Rama back in April. Guy named Taj. In a million years, I never would have guessed that—"

"Is Taj in Duna?"

"No. He fought with Rayad. Still stuck in Camp Peace."

"But you're sure he helped with Rama?"

"Sure as sure. Sure as I can be," he slurred.

"Are you sick?"

"No, I'm drunk."

"Erkan—"

"No worries. Just a liiiiittle drunk. Tipped the bottle this morning." He laughed. "After almost two months! Shame on me." The raspy sound of his weak laughter made me sick inside.

"Wish you hadn't."

"Me too. Now, do you want to talk with Taj?"

"You said he was in Camp Peace."

"Video call. We'll do a video call, the three of us. You can hear the story from him face to face. Screen to screen." He laughed again. "Want to talk with Taj now?"

"Erkan, I'm on the farm."

"So am I."

"What?" I jumped to my feet and scanned the hillside above me, the footpath from the house to the barn, Rama's juniper thicket, dusty and yellowed from the dry summer past. No Erkan.

"Joking. I'm joking. But my car's parked down at the turnoff to your road. With me inside."

***

At the front door, Erkan slipped off his shoes and placed them by the bench. The walk uphill in the cool air seemed to have cleared his head some, but he still swayed as he straightened and grabbed at the wall for support. When he tried to hang his yellow jacket on the coat-hooks, a hat of Arjun's fell to the floor. He cursed.

"Let me." I stooped to grab the hat and we almost bumped heads.

He followed me into the sitting room, rubbing his hands together nervously. "So you do have electricity. The way they talk in Dor about people up here, you'd think..." His voice trailed away.

"We have the generator for the lights, but we heat with wood. Kitchen stove runs on a gas bottle."

He rubbed his hands across his face. "This is not what I came to talk about. Sorry, I'm not feeling myself today. Do I seem a little off to you?"

"You said you'd been drinking."

"Oh, yes, I did, didn't I? Ha. Which reminds me—do you think it's a good idea for me to be here? Don't want to get trampled by that prize bull of yours."

I bit my lip. "Kiva's not here."

Quit talking before you shame yourself, I wanted to tell him. Instead I said, "I'll get you some tea. Do you like milk in it?"

He snorted. "Milk? No. Milk tea is for cowherds."

I brought in the tea and some leftover ginger cake and set it on the side table.

He tapped his phone's screen to put it on Speaker.

A man answered in Sev. "Hello? Erkan, right?"

Sitabi wandered in with both hands full of toy trains. She sat down, hooked them together, and started chugging the little cars round and round on the rag rug. Her whistle sound effects were so loud I couldn't hear what Taj said at first, except that it was in Sev. Erkan said he'd try a video call.

I sat down beside him on the cushioned bench by the fireplace and Erkan held the phone out so we could both see the screen.

Taj's face bobbed up and down, like he was trying to adjust the angle of his phone for better light. He sat inside a tent, one of those gray Camp Peace tents. Behind his head, the reverse image of the European League's blue logo shone faintly through the plastic wall. Taj wasn't near as good-looking as Kiva, but they had the same green eyes.

"Do you speak Tur?" I asked.

"Of course," he said in Tur. He had a Dor accent, but the word "KILLER" was tattooed down his neck in the Anglo script only the mountain Tur still used.

Sufya stuck her head in through the door, a puzzled look on her face. She caught sight of Erkan and disappeared again.

"So..." I began, and stopped. Maybe Taj would have a better idea of how this conversation should go.

"You're Rama Enda's wife?" he asked.

In the background, a woman's shrill voice called out in Sev.

"Not now, Bina!" Taj snapped. "I'm on the phone. So when we learned that Rama had been killed, our militia commander—he's dead now too—sent me and a half-Tur guy named Igor to retrieve the body. Rama's body, I mean."

Taj kept fidgeting like his seat was uncomfortable. Probably it was. Most people hadn't taken chairs or sofas when they were evacuated from Dor.

"We brought him in a car to Klim that same night. Wrapped the body in plastic so it wouldn't stink so bad—"

Erkan made a small sound in his throat.

Taj scowled. "She wants the story, right? I'm giving her the story. Since he had a Tur Kej ID card, we decided we'd bury him outside Dor province if we could. Sometimes we'd go as far as one of the cemetaries near the border towns."

"Moltoy?" I asked.

"No, we didn't get as far north as that. Petrol was getting low, so we had to turn around. It was me, and three others who went. We ended up burying him a ways off the road on the Tur Kej side just after we crossed the border. Border police don't patrol that road much on either side."

Sadness filled my chest and sat there, cold and heavy. "You just dug a hole by the road?"

He shrugged. "Pretty much. But he lies in Tur dirt. Isn't that what he would have wanted?"

"Yes," I whispered.

Erkan put his arm around my shoulders softly, like he was afraid I'd move away if I noticed.

"It was a bare stretch of ground. Rocky. There was a clump of junipers not too far away, " Taj said.

"Juniper trees? Really?" That made me smile, though my throat ached from holding back tears.

Taj laughed. "They're not exactly rare. I noticed because it was a big clump. And..." Taj thought for a moment, biting his thumbnail. "There were so many rocks lying around we built a mound over the grave."

"What prayers did you say?" I asked.

"I didn't say any prayers, that's for sure!" He laughed. "Listen, lady, we were doing this nearly every week. Didn't have time."

"I understand."

His hard face softened for a moment. "Rama was a Rayad brother. You do what you have to do for your brothers."

I nodded. Tried to say 'Thank you,' but found I couldn't speak.

"Wait a minute." Taj held up a finger. "Somebody had a little Rayad flag that he stuck in the top of the mound. I think it was Igor. But I don't remember for sure, and Igor's dead now, too."

"I'm sorry," I said.

"It is what it is." Taj looked away and waved at someone I couldn't see. "Get over here. I'm done."

The call cut off.

Erkan cursed softly. "I'll call him back."

I closed my eyes and remembered the tangy smell of junipers with the sun on them and Rama's rare, shy smile. "No. It's all right. If you talk to Taj again, tell him thank you from me."

Erkan's jaw set. "I highly doubt I'll talk to him again. In fact, if it wasn't for you, I wouldn't have called him in the first place."

"Why?"

"Long story." He reached for his tea glass for the first time and took a long drink as if to say, 'No more questions.'

"Thanks for your help," I said. "Knowing...it's taken such a weight off my mind."

He turned toward me, tilting his head to see me better. "You knowing where Rama's grave is, or Kiva knowing about how Rama died?"

"I think...maybe both."

"Maybe." He nodded. "When you met me at the door today, I wouldn't have guessed you were the same woman as the one I took to see Rais Padmi. There's light in your eyes again."

I looked down at Sitabi lying on her stomach on the floor at my feet so as to be on a level with her train.

"Go play on the rug, Baby Girl. The wood will give you splinters." She ignored me, like usual.

"Oh, by the way," Erkan said, "I gave Sanjit a call yesterday. He knows he'd be wise to go chase his dreams elsewhere."

"That's good," I said. Now Kiva wouldn't have to get himself mixed up in the Sinds' business at all.

Erkan stood and pushed the phone into his back pocket. "It's been a delightful visit, but I'd better be going." He started for the door, almost tripping over Sitabi's train. She jerked it out of the way and glared up at him.

"How did you come to be friends with Sanjit in the first place?" I asked. Ever since the three of us met at the abandoned apartments that day back in April, I'd wondered.

"We met in Camp Peace after the evacuation." He stopped, and studied the dotted lines on the backs of his hands. "And yes, I knew what he was doing. Not proud of that. But he showed me how to get out of the camp. And he had really good ink."

"Which is all that matters in life," I said, putting out my tongue at him.

Erkan stared at me for a moment, then laughed. "Exactly."

"And the reason I was in Pasha the day we met you—believe it or not, I was looking for my sister's cat, Coco. As for what Sanjit was up to, well, I didn't ask, and he didn't tell."

"Did you find him?"

"Coco? No."

"I thought you hated Sanjit now. Didn't think you'd warn him about the kill order."

"Well," Erkan shrugged. "I don't know. He got Dunya and the baby out of Camp Peace."

"He did?"

"Long story."

"You said that before."

"All stories are long."

I grabbed Mother's red shawl off the hook beside Erkan's jacket and we went out to his car together.

He watched me take in the vodka bottles scattered in the back seat, the dirty clothing, the stained seat cushions.

"I'm mostly sober these days."

"Then why—"

He stuffed his hands into his pockets, making the cheap yellow fabric crackle. "Except for when I'm not."

I shook my head. He thought his drinking didn't hurt nobody but himself. Why couldn't he see he was wrong?

"I'm leaving soon," he said.

I glanced at his car. "So...?"

"I mean leaving Sevia. The Canadian government is running a visa lottery for Tur victims of war crimes from this conflict. Dr. Neyrev suggested I apply, so I did. Mrs. Neyrev helped me write up my case in English and submit it. And I won."

I gasped. "You're going to Canada?"

"Yes. Seems kind of like cheating though, since I don't remember much of what happened to me. At least not when I'm awake."

"I thought other countries weren't taking anybody who'd been part of Rayad."

"The countries in the European League ruled against it, but Canada's not a European League country. But they might change their minds when they see what a threat to national security I am!" He flexed his arms and threw out his narrow chest.

When I tried to smile, it felt fake. I wasn't sure if I should be sorry or glad. "Canada's a long way off."

"Indeed it is. Maybe that's a good thing."

"When are you leaving?"

"In less than a month, if all goes according to plan."

A loud squeal from Sitabi cut him off. She raced barefoot across the dusty yard toward us, a train car clutched in each hand.

"Mama! They came apart!" She pushed them at me. "Hook them together!"

I took the little red cars and slid the metal hook through the loop. "There." I handed them back. "Now get inside. It's too cold to be out here barefoot."

Sitabi drew her dark eyebrows together. "But you're barefoot."

Erkan chuckled.

I gave him a look and turned back to Sitabi. "I'm grown. When you get grown you can run around barefoot, too."

She tiptoed back to the house, holding her trains out in front of her so they'd stay together.

"When we met at the fair, I already knew I'd be leaving for Canada soon," Erkan said quietly, looking after Sitabi. "I shouldn't say this—it was a completely idiotic idea—but I was going to ask you to come with me."

I froze, staring at him. What to say? "You...were?"

"Yes." He took a long breath. " Of course it was crazy—much better for you to stay here with your family. And Kiva. I shouldn't even have thought for one second about asking you to give all this up." He waved a hand around us at the farmhouse, the almost-bare beech trees, the hill. "But I love you, Preen. I've loved you since always and I'd hate to leave you behind if I thought you weren't happy."

I pressed my hands to my ears. "Erkan, no. Stop. Please stop."

Why couldn't he have kept pretending that he was just a good friend until he went off to Canada? Maybe if he'd stayed sober a few more weeks, he would have.

"I'm sorry." He bowed his head and rubbed the sleeve of his jacket across his face. "I shouldn't have said anything. Forget it, please."

"Don't say sorry. I'm the one who's sorry. I wish—" He'd saved my life and my only thanks was to give him more pain. But what else did he expect?

My eyes filled, and his yellow jacket blurred into two. I wiped tears away with the end of Mother's shawl. "I hope you like it in Canada."

"Sure." He gave me his crooked smile.

The breeze carried a rooster's crow down the hill toward us. Out of the corner of my eye, I saw Mother's green dress fluttering in the wind as she walked up the path from the barn, a milk jug on her shoulder.

"Your Kiva would be a wonderful guy, if he wasn't so full of himself," Erkan said. "You'll be good for him."

He opened the car door and climbed in, stabbed the key into the ignition and started the engine. As he reached for the gearshift, the bottle of vodka he'd wedged between the seats tipped over and spilled onto the passenger's side floor mat. He swore and fumbled to right it.

"Dump it out," I said softly, but he didn't seem to hear.

"Oh! Almost forgot." He pulled a leather wallet from his jacket pocket and handed me a twenty-dinar note. "Will you give that to Kiva for me? And remind him that tattoos last a lifetime, so choose the artist carefully."

Chapter Nineteen: Kiva

I'd planned to visit Dr. Neyrev when I was at the hospital, but I ended up not even seeing him.

Down in the waiting room, I found Mrs. Neyrev and Arjun sat together by the window in those sticky vinyl chairs. Mrs Neyrev had her hand on Arjun's knee and he kept patting it, like he was soothing a baby. They told me Dr. Neyrev was asleep and the doctor said he shouldn't be disturbed. I gave them the bread and apples and thermos of milk tea Preen's mother had sent, and headed back to the Rastikar farm in my truck.

Since the tires looked a little low, I stopped by the gas station on the way back and got them pumped up in preparation for our trip to Moltoy.

I hadn't told Preen beforehand, but I'd decided to stop by the Sind farm, too. Next time Preen brought it up, I could casually mention I'd already spoken with the Sinds and take that weight off her mind, at least. It didn't seem right that Sanjit should get away free to Tur Fen, but it seemed even less right that he should be hunted down and killed without ever getting a trial or a chance to speak for himself.

I'd never understood the Neyrevs' request that the man who'd stabbed their son not be turned over to the police. Now that I found myself in a similar situation, their choice was beginning to make sense.

Back in Dor, the police weren't nothing more than a bunch of White Horse thugs, and any Tur—let alone any Rayad member—would be lucky to get to prison alive. Now Alexander's killer might walk free, but Dr. Neyrev could take comfort in the fact that he hadn't sent a man to his death without first hearing his side of the story.

The track to the Sinds' farmhouse lay between two low hills. No telling how long since they'd put gravel down—it was so pitted and washed-out that I'd have had a smoother ride through the pasture.

The farm itself was just as bad. The house and barn had both been dark green once, but the paint had faded and peeled away in big patches, showing warped, rotten siding beneath. A hole gaped in one corner of the barn where big pieces of the sheet metal roofing had slipped off, like a snake casting its skin.

I parked beside the rusty skeleton of a tractor with hay baler still attached and started for the house. Even in the sunshine, it looked a miserable place—saggy front porch and broken windowpanes stuffed with towels.

Clumps of brown grass, mixed with thistles, stood knee-deep in the house yard. Nothing stirred except for the wind breathing through the weeds. I missed the sounds of a live farm—generators rumbling, cattle lowing, hired men yelling to each other. Maybe Manish and Rani couldn't afford farm help anymore.

Back in the spring, Arjun had gone to help Manish out when his hired hand broke his leg at the start of calving season. Shame on me that I hadn't gone, too. I'd been so took up with Preen running off at the beginning of April, I hadn't thought much on what trouble our neighbors might be facing. Not long after, Manish had gotten sick, and as far as I knew, he hadn't been about since.

"Hello?" I called, knocking on the front door. "Manish? Rani? Sanjit? Anybody home?"

No answer. I crossed the creaky porch and peered in through the window. The kitchen looked stale, like nobody had used it for a day or two.

A skinny orange cat came streaking around the corner, leapt off the porch and disappeared into the grass. I spun round so fast I almost fell over. When the jitters stopped running up and down my spine, I crossed the yard. Stepping over the rail fence on the far side, I headed toward the barn. In spite of what I'd told Preen, I was not easy in my mind about meeting Sanjit, especially if the meeting ended up being just the two of us.

The big double doors stood open. I walked inside. "Hello? Sanjit, you here?"

Pigeons rustled on the beams overhead. A couple fluttered down to the floor, hoping I'd brought grain, maybe. Hay dust drifted down from the loft above like thin smoke.

I sensed movement behind me, and looked around.

A dark-haired man about my age took a step forward through the doorway and stopped dead. His face turned almost as gray as the dirty shirt under his jacket. The cannister he held dropped from his hand and tipped over. Clear liquid gushed out, and the reek of kerosene filled the barn, blotting out the smell of moldy straw.

"Hey," I said, "You're Sanjit, right? Manish and Rani's nephew?"

"Yes...?" He made it sound more like a question than an answer.

I hadn't gotten a chance to get a good look at Sanjit last time we met, because he was shooting at me. But this had to be him. Medium height. Thin. Brown dreadlocks bound with wire nested on the top of his head. And a look of blank terror on his face that slowly changed into an expression I couldn't read.

We stood for a minute, sizing each other up.

Sanjit spoke first. "It's a good place, this farm. Just a little run-down."

I nodded, since my mouth had gone dry.

"All it needed was some time and money." Without taking his eyes off me, he bent and picked up the cannister.

"Watch it with that kerosene, man! You're going to burn the place down."

"So?" He upended the cannister and the last bit of kerosene came gurgling out onto the floorboards. He threw the cannister into a corner. "It's my place. I can do what I want with it."

"You can't go sloshing kerosene around the—"

He waved for me to be quiet. "Uncle Manish died Friday night. And Aunt Rani's with her people in town. It's my place now."

"Better poor and alive than rich and dead," I said. "Which is why I came—"

"Poor and alive, rich and dead," he mocked. "How true." His lips curled back showing the missing incisors. So Sanjit was somebody's eldest son.

"If you have any sense you'll—"

"Sanjit Sind, rich and dead. How many men can say they had a big farm and a death sentence come to them in the same night?" He laughed softly—an ugly sound.

Did he already know Rais Padmi had ordered him killed? Who would have told him?

I tried again. "I came to warn you—"

"You're Preen's man, aren't you?" Sanjit's dark eyes narrowed as he studied my face. "I saw you with her at the clothing store."

"So what if I am? Your trouble is your trouble. Got nothing to do with me, or her."

"Not true," he said. "Unfortunately for you." One hand went into his coat and came out with a little handgun made of some dark, slick metal.

My heart jumped into my throat. "Hey, put that back. I never did you wrong."

"Preen Enda's new boyfriend, of all people." His smile wasn't a smile—just a baring of the teeth. "Makes me think God hasn't forgotten me after all." He pointed that little gun of his at my chest.

When Preen had been with me, I'd charged him without a second thought, gun or no gun. Alone, I lost my head, turned and ran for the big window at the back of the barn instead.

His pistol cracked. A bullet punched through the barn wall just ahead of me. I jumped for the windowsill, missed, hit a rotten place in the floor, and crashed down through it, bringing handfuls of dry-rotted wood with me.

Two meters or so down I hit packed earth. I'd tried to break my fall with my right arm, and it somehow ended up twisted beneath me. Pain shot from my wrist to my shoulder. For a minute I lay on my stomach, wheezing for breath as sparks danced behind my eyes.

I felt my arm up and down. Couldn't tell if it was broken or not, but it sure hurt enough to be broken. I couldn't hardly move my fingers. I got to my knees and squinted up at the jagged hole I'd made. If I stood upright, my head would almost touch the floor which was now my ceiling.

Sanjit bent to look down inside. His shape blocked out the light.

I scrambled as far back under the floor as I could go.

"Come out, you," he called down. "Preen's man, if you're alive down there, come out."

Since I was alive, and planned to stay alive, I stayed put.

Sanjit couldn't see me, but he started shooting into the hole anyway. Crack! Crack! Crack! I lay flat as I could, with my back against the barn's stone foundation wall and my good arm over my head, shaking like a dead leaf.

After a minute or two, he moved away, muttering to himself, something about, "Didn't think she'd do me like this."

Did he mean Preen? He couldn't possibly know she'd let his name fall at the Council House. Maybe he'd have laid the blame on her no matter who found him out. His hatred of Rama hadn't faded when Rama died, it just spread to hurt the people Rama cared about.

The floorboards groaned as Sanjit crossed them, walking back and forth through the barn inches above my head. He seemed to be carrying on a one-man argument with somebody named Mosin. A metal cannister rang as he threw it against the wall.

I gave him time to get well away from the hole, then pulled out my phone. The screen had cracked, but the flashlight still worked. I got up, turned it on and shone its beam around the underground room.

Against the near wall lay a bag full of soft lumps that might once have been potatoes and the worm-eaten carcass of a rat. The light on my phone caught the eyes of a couple of live ones on the far side. Those tiny red balls glaring back started me shivering all over again.

I brushed off wood fragments and hay dust and started scanning the ceiling for a trap door. If they used to store root crops down here, there had to be one.

But what if Sanjit found it first and was waiting for me on the other side?

I cradled my throbbing wrist against my chest and stood still for a minute, thinking. Even if I did find a trap door, I couldn't hoist myself up one-handed. Maybe I could find a ladder or a couple of crates, or something I could use to climb out. I started toward the other end of the cellar, moving as quiet as I could.

A dry, bitter smell began to fill the place. The dust in the air seemed to be getting thicker, catching in my throat and burning my eyes. Took me a minute or two to realize it wasn't dust, but smoke.

Chapter Twenty: Kiva

When I found the trap door, I reached up and pushed it with my good arm, but couldn't raise it. Casting about for something to lever it up with, I stumbled over a long pole half-buried under a pile of feed sacks against the wall. They'd probably used the pole to prop the trap door open for ventilation when they stored potatoes down here. I lifted it clumsily with one hand and tried to shove the door open. Didn't budge it an inch. They must have parked a tractor overtop of it, or a generator, or something. What to do?

I'd have thought twice about coming to the Sind farm if I'd suspected Sanjit would decide to send his future up in smoke around us. At least I hadn't asked anybody to come along with me. The thought of what might have happened if I'd brought Arjun, or my sweet Preen, sent chills down my back.

We'd have been safer if we'd let Rais Padmi's people deal with Sanjit after all. But safer didn't mean better. Didn't mean right.

Even though I stood trapped under the floor in the reek and heat, I couldn't feel that I'd been foolish to warn Sanjit of his danger. If he'd listened to me, he'd have lost the farm, but escaped with his life—justice and forgiveness both.

All the same, I was in big trouble.

The pain from my arm made my head spin, and the smoke that leaked down through the floor ate into my throat and eyes like hot pepper. With the smoke this bad below, it had to be twice as thick above. Sanjit must have left the barn. I could phone for help without fear of him hearing me. I slid to the ground, leaning back against the wall.

My mobile phone signal showed only one bar. Coverage wasn't very good outside of Duna, and being underground didn't improve it any. Holding the phone stable against my knee with my injured wrist, I dialed the Emergency Department code with the other hand. The call failed. My phone slipped to the ground and I fumbled to pick it up again.

The pain in my arm blurred everything, turned my stomach sour, made the simplest things like where to tap on a phone screen seem almost impossible. Or maybe the smoke in my lungs did it. My fingers moved like they were wrapped in thick bandages.

Call back. Call failed. Call back. Call failed. Oh, God...

That little lone signal bar disappeared. My heart sank.

Gritting my teeth, I stood on tiptoe right under the hole I'd broken in the floor. Didn't seem like that would make much difference, but I got one bar again. I called Arjun. He didn't answer.

As panic built like steam inside me, I paced the cellar on shaky legs. What if I couldn't get out? What if the barn fell in? What if I died down here? Would my family ever find my bones? Oh God, give me one more call...

Chapter Twenty-One: Preen

Not ten minutes after Erkan left, my phone rang and Kiva's picture flashed onto the screen. I'd snapped that photo of him a few weeks before—caught him mid-yawn—eyes closed, mouth wide. When I showed him I'd used it for his caller ID, he about fell over laughing.

I took my phone away from Sitabi, who'd lost interest in her train and started fiddling with it.

"Are you headed home yet?" I asked. "Did you get to speak to the Neyrevs?"

A buzz of static. Silence.

"Kiva, can you hear me?" I stood and started for the front door for a better connection outside.

"Preen, call the..." A loud hissing noise cut Kiva off before he said more, but that raw, scared voice made my stomach cold.

"What's wrong?"

".... the Emergency Department." He started coughing worse than Dr. Neyrev. "Preen, call the....I'm not getting through....fire..." Static blotted out the rest.

I squeezed the phone to my ear like that would help me hear him better, fumbling at the doorknob with my other hand.

Sitabi followed me, holding out her hands for the phone. "Please, I want it," she whined. "I was playing with it."

"Quiet!" I pulled the door open and stepped outside. Her little face crumpled and she started to cry.

"Kiva, what's wrong? Where are you?" I shouted into the phone.

"...Sind farm." Kiva gasped. "I'm stuck in the barn....the floor... call the..."

"Kiva?"

Silence. I looked at my phone. His picture was gone.

The terrible fear in Kiva's voice gave me the shakes so bad the phone almost slipped from my hand.

Questions raced through my mind. How did the fire start? Why should Kiva be in the Sinds' old barn? Where was Sanjit in all of this?

Chapter Twenty-Two: Kiva

I beat on the rotten boards above me with the pole until it got too heavy to hold and slipped from my hand. "Help!" I yelled. "Help! I'm stuck down here!"

No answer—only the hiss and crackle of fire burning through the Sinds' winter stock of hay. I shouted and screamed until my voice was gone and my throat as dry as the dust. Even if no one heard me, sitting quiet in the dark, waiting to die, was more than I could bear.

Again and again I jumped for the hole and caught the crumbling wood at the edge with one hand, only to have it break away. I staggered back and forth, kicking the stone walls until I couldn't stand. Then I crawled around the edges of the cellar, seeking a weak spot or an opening in the foundation stones. There had to be one somewhere, or the draft wouldn't be pulling so much smoke down.

The heat from the fire above smothered like a wool blanket in July. At least the packed earth and the foundation walls stayed cool. Close to the ground, the air seemed better, too. I pulled off my jacket and shirt, hissing with pain as the sleeve wrenched my hurt arm. I lifted my undershirt and held the damp cloth over my mouth and nose to keep some of the smoke out.

A single gunshot cracked outside. My heart leaped into my throat. I waited for footsteps, for Sanjit's voice. Maybe he'd brave the smoke to finish me off, after all.

Minutes passed. Nothing happened. I collapsed onto my stomach and lay in the dirt with sweat dripping off me.

God, don't let me die. Please.

The dim brown light faded to black.

Chapter Twenty-Three: Preen

I flung open the kitchen door. Mother stood by the sink, pouring the big jug of milk into jars to skim for cream.

"I've got to go—Kiva needs me," I gasped.

Milk sloshed down the front of her dark-green dress as she spun around, her eyes and mouth going wide with surprise. "What's wrong?"

Already halfway to the front door, I called over my shoulder. "Don't let Sitabi get into trouble."

"Preen!"

I ignored her and kept running. When I had Kiva home safe, he could explain everything.

The quickest way to the Sinds' farm was to climb the hill behind our house and cut across the pastureland between. I scrambled up the steep slope, over broken rock, past sparse clumps of juniper and thorn. Spears of dried grass poked the plastic shoes I'd grabbed on the way out the door. Never in my eighteen years had I climbed that hill so fast, and never had it seemed so far to the top.

At the top I stopped, panting, and looked around. Below me to the right ran a gentler slope, cut in two halfway down by a barbed-wire fence, the boundary between the Sinds' pastureland and ours. A column of smoke rose from behind the next hill to meet the gray clouds of the sky—hot black smoke.

I choked down a scream and leaped down the slope. The faster my heart beat, the slower my legs moved, like in those dreams where you have to run and you just can't.

"Kiva, where are you?" I shouted.

Grazing cattle raised their heads to look at me as I ran past, sharp grass whipping my ankles. My scared thoughts ran even faster. Had Sanjit lost his head and set his own farm on fire? Had Kiva somehow been trapped? Duna was only a couple of miles to the south, but how quick could the Emergency Department people get their fire trucks up here?

If there's more trouble to come because of what I did, let it only come on me, I prayed silently as I ran.

I slowed again when I got to the low place at the bottom of the slope. Water usually gathered there after a rain, and the last thing I needed was to slip in mud and sprain an ankle. At best, it was a half hour's walk from our place to the Sinds' across the hills, and longer by the road. A barn could burn to the ground in that time. A man could die in a tenth of that time.

Why had I thought I'd finished paying for my foolish ways? Maybe the family didn't hold nothing against me anymore. Maybe God had listened to my prayers. But if forgiveness didn't mean I was free from my past, it seemed pretty poor comfort.

I looked around, pressing the stitch in my side. Down the hill to the left, Sanjit's horse stood in the shelter of a clump of trees, near a few of our cows. The horse stood a head taller than any of them and was as white and bony as they were dark and sleek. It must have gotten lonely and hopped over a low place in the fence.

An idea struck me. Wiping away the tears the wind had streaked across my face, I walked up to the horse, slow, so it wouldn't get scared. It wore an old halter, the kind with a ring underneath you can hook a lead to—no reins or real bridle, of course. I'd ridden horses bareback before, but never without reins.

"Hey," I whispered. "That's a good horse."

It looked to be old, with hollow cheeks and silver hairs sprinkled in the gray of its muzzle. Those big, gentle eyes rolled toward me. Its floppy lips blew hot air over my outstretched hand. I reached for its halter and drew his head around.

"This way now." I guided it over toward a tree that had come down last winter, climbed onto the trunk, and hoisted myself onto its warm, slippery back. It snorted again, but didn't seem to mind. I grabbed two fistfuls of the mane and kicked its sides.

"Come on, now. We need to be fast."

It started at a trot. As the slope spread out below us it changed to a canter, then, for an exciting, terrifying moment, we were galloping, hooves clattering over the rocky ground. Faster, faster, I urged Sanjit's horse inside my head. Across the valley we clattered, sending little rocks and puffs of dust flying. Up the next hill, over the top, down the far slope. The brisk wind drove smoke toward us, making the horse skittish.

As we came up within shouting distance of their house, I saw Kiva's truck parked out front. He was still somewhere on the Sinds' place—no question about it. He wouldn't leave that truck for anything.

The horse tossed its head and veered off toward the hill again. I leaned forward, rubbing its nose, coaxing it around. "Easy, easy, it's all right."

When it slowed to a walk I slid off and ran toward the shouting and the smoke.

The Emergency Department had sent an ambulance and a tank truck up from Duna. They must have arrived just a few minutes before I did. Both vehicles stood in the flat area in front of the Sinds' house, but farther back than Kiva's truck, to be safe from flying sparks.

Four men braced themselves against the big orange hose that shot a jet of water as thick as my leg at the flames that came licking out the windows. As water hit the blaze, huge puffs of steam and smoke rose into the sky. Manish and Rani's house was pretty near gone. Had they gotten out in time? Where was Kiva? Where was Sanjit?

A District Security truck with the black Bull's Horns on the side came bumping up the Sinds' drive and parked beside the ambulance. Two more men jumped out.

I'd told the woman on the line at the Emergency Department that Kiva was trapped in the barn, but all the ED workers seemed to be gathered around the house. The smoke billowed too thick to see if the barn was also on fire, or even if it still stood.

My heart hammered against my breastbone as I stumbled across the house yard, half-choked by smoke and dust. "There's a man in the barn!" I screamed. "Check the barn!"

Chapter Twenty-Four: Kiva

Somewhere outside, in the cool air and sunshine, a siren whooped once and a heavy vehicle skidded to a stop. Another drove slowly past the barn entrance, its engine vibrating through the floor. Far as I could tell it stopped too and stood idling close by. The Emergency Department's Fire Division trucks must have arrived.

Doors slammed. A man's voice yelled, "Get a hose on the house—we'll check the barn."

A diesel engine revved. The shrill beep of a truck in reverse cut through the smoke swirling in my brain.

"Help!" My voice wouldn't go louder than a whisper. I tried to stand but my legs didn't work. They'd grown numb, and heavy as lead. My arms tingled too, but the one I'd injured didn't hurt near as bad as it had before.

"Hello?" a man yelled. "Anybody in here? Have them bring a hose this way."

Above me, something hit the barn floor with a thump. Then came a whoosh like when a kettle boils over onto the fire, except ten times louder.

"Under the floor!" I tried to scream. It came out a thin, faint whistle.

"Check the stalls in the back," the same voice called. "We'll try the loft when this fire's under control."

God, let them find the hole. Let them realize I'm down here.

The floor shook under pounding boots and scalding-hot water began dripping down onto me through the cracks in the boards. Once again, darkness rose up behind my eyes and everything went quiet.

Chapter Twenty-Five: Preen

I stopped dead. The shout I'd drawn breath for came out a whimper. On the far side of the tank truck, something—a body—lay huddled on the ground, covered by a red-and-gray striped blanket. A District Security officer bent over it.

I started toward him. The other officer stepped in front of me and I ran straight into his big, soft belly. The strangled noise that burst out of me didn't even sound human, more like a cat crying in the night.

"Kiva!" I screamed. "Kiva!" The man wrapped his arms around me and started backing me away from the body by the trucks, gentle but firm. My plastic shoes kicked and skidded over the dusty ground.

"My fiance— was stuck in the barn—where is he now?" I choked out. "Is that him?"

"You don't want to go over there," he said. "You don't want to see that."

A group of ED workers gathered round me. The officer who'd caught me sat me down on the ground, held my thrashing hands. "Ma'am, listen to me. Ma'am," he said over and over till I had to breathe and look up at him.

"I had no idea anybody but the old couple lived here," someone said. "Are you their daughter?"

"No. I'm Preen Enda from the farm over that way." I jerked my head back up toward the hill. "I'm the one who called about the fire. My fiance came here this morning to talk to the Sinds. Where is he now?" Ash caught in my throat and I started coughing so hard I couldn't hardly breathe.

The fire had to be Sanjit's doing. He must have decided that if he couldn't have the farm, nobody would. But how did Kiva end up trapped in a burning barn?

"I'm so sorry." The Security Officer looked up at one of the firefighters who stood above me. "The Sinds are safe. We checked the house and barn and they were both empty. Nobody inside. But I'm afraid..." his eyes flashed to the striped blanket.

Oh no.

His mouth kept moving, but no sound came out. The wind fluttered his big gray moustache.

So Kiva was gone. Like my father. Like Rama. I was the Moon-girl in that old story, with everybody I loved turning to dust at my touch.

'God is kind,' Arjun had told me since we were little. 'Yes, our father's dead of a brain tumor, but God is kind. Yes, I got beat up on the way home from work last night, but God is kind. Yes, the man you love won't come home no more, but God is kind.'

I heard him in my head, steady as a clock—sticking my fingers in my ears didn't shut out his soft voice. How could he be right?

One of the ED workers cleared his throat. "Miss Enda," he said, looking at his boots. "I don't know if it's a comfort, but he didn't die in the fire. He was already gone by the time it took the house."

"What?" My eyes and throat burned.

"It was quick and painless—a gunshot to the head."

Sanjit shot him?

"No!" I scrambled to my feet. Men out of their minds with evil belonged in Dor, not in our quiet hills. "No, that can't be. That just can't be."

I kept saying that, but deep down I knew it could be—if Sanjit wanted Kiva dead for some reason, it didn't have to make sense.

A man put his hands on my shoulders and tried to ease me back to the ground. Another handed me a water bottle. Dirty orange coveralls and serious, sympathetic faces blurred before my eyes.

"Try to drink something," the old Security Officer said. "This smoke is hard on the lungs."

"Dear God, why did Sanjit shoot him?" I screamed in his face.

The answer came almost as quick as the question and it turned my stomach cold. Because of me. Sanjit wouldn't have had no quarrel with

Kiva if not for me. Now Rama and Kiva were both dead and I was to blame.

Did that mean I'd passed beyond where kindness could reach?

One of the other men whispered something to the Security Officer and made like he was holding the barrel of a pistol under his chin.

The ED worker who had spoken first scowled at the both of them and shook his head. He took off his helmet. Underneath, the bandana tying up his dreadlocks had turned almost black with sweat and soot. His orange coveralls were soaked with water from the hose.

"I'm so sorry for your loss," he said. "But I promise he felt no pain. He—"

I grabbed his arm. "Let me see him."

The ED worker shook his head. "Trust me, you don't want to see him."

"No. I have to see him. That's my Kiva!"

"Wait, wait," another man called. He came running up, waving his hands. "What did you say? Kiva who?"

"Kiva Manjali. My fiance." I clenched my jaw to stop it trembling. Why had God brought my foolishness down on Kiva's head? If Sitabi and me were alone again—oh, what would we ever do?

"I know Kiva Manjali," he said. "The dead man we found on the front porch—I don't know who he is, but he's definitely not Kiva."

I jumped up, gasping like they'd turned the fire hose on me. "The front porch?"

"Yes. We didn't see anybody else. The place is—"

I sprinted for the barn.

They yelled and took off after me, but they couldn't none of them catch me before I got there.

The barn had caught fire too, but it wasn't burned near as bad as the house. Water ran down blackened wood, forming puddles around the foundation. Piles of soaked, charred hay reeked like a hundred years of hot summer days.

"Kiva!" I yelled. "Kiva, where are you?"

Chapter Twenty-Six: Kiva

"Kiva!"

A scream cut through the roaring in my ears.

"Kiva!" Preen's voice, crying my name over and over again.

For a minute I couldn't decide if I was awake or dreaming. I opened my eyes. The cellar was hazy with smoke and as hot as standing inside the fireplace.

How am I still alive? I thought. Arjun must have been praying for me today.

Slowly I got to my knees, whimpering with pain when my hurt arm jarred against the ground. Slowly I crawled over to the smoky light streaming down through the hole.

Down here under the floor! I yelled inside my mind, but nothing much came out of my mouth.

Moving slow as an old lady I peeled off my undershirt and tossed it up at the hole. It caught on the ragged wood, hung for a second, and fell back on top of my head. I dragged it off and tossed again. Made it. Would they notice a dirty, wadded-up shirt on the floor of a dark barn? With my arm bent back like I'd grown a second elbow, I couldn't hardly think straight for pain.

Footsteps creaked here and there above me.

"We checked before, when we put the fire out," a man's voice called. "It's empty. No animals, even."

"Please..." I waited. Kicked at the stone foundation wall with a boot that barely made a noise. "Help."

My voice was lost in the clatter of boots and squeaking of old wood.

One of the floorboards above me cracked and shifted down a hand-breadth. Somebody yelped and scrambled back. "Look out! The floor's rotten under that window." The footsteps moved away, got fainter. "Could have been a nasty fall."

"He's in here somewhere," Preen said, in a voice ragged with shouting. "He told me he was."

"Wait a minute." Somebody stopped a few meters away from my hole. "Where'd this shirt come from? It's not burned at all."

"Help," I whispered. "Please, help." I struggled to my feet, took a step or two, and fell. The fresh shock of pain when my arm bent underneath me forced out a groan.

Preen's voice sounded right above me, squealing as shrill as Sitabi. "I found him. I found him. He's under the floor. He's alive!"

I lay on my face, whispering thanks into the dirt while they tore away the rotten floorboards and eased a ladder down.

Two of the ED men climbed down into the cellar with me, almost glowing in those orange coverall suits of theirs. They hoisted me up the ladder, carried me out of the barn, and laid me on a blanket beside the ambulance. When they strapped an oxygen mask over my face, I lay back in their arms, closed my eyes, and spent some time breathing.

Shameful as it was to be lying on the ground filthy and half-naked in front of my fiancee and most of Duna's Emergency Department, at that moment I didn't care.

The ED fellows offered to put me in the ambulance, but I didn't want to move just then. The fresh, chilly wind dried my sweat and blew life back into me. After a minute I started shaking so bad my teeth rattled.

They told me they could set and wrap my broken arm on the spot, but I'd need to go to the hospital for a proper cast. I told them maybe later.

After they set the bone, Preen knelt beside me and wrapped a blanket around my shoulders. Her face was streaked with soot and tears, but her eyes shone.

She looked triumphant, like the time I'd dared her to eat an apple the ants had found and she'd done it—ants and all.

"You're alive," she whispered, touching my face, my hair, my shoulder. "You're all right. You're safe."

"Thanks to you." I squeezed her hand and smiled.

The fuzz had cleared out of my head, but my body still felt too stiff and heavy to be mine. "If you hadn't come when you did..." I stopped to catch my breath. "I don't know how much longer I'd have lasted down there."

"I knew you were in there somewhere," Preen said, halfway between smiling and crying."I knew it!"

She jumped to her feet and danced around me in those cracked plastic shoes, snapping her fingers, her shining face tipped up to the sky. She danced like her heart would burst if she sat still.

A middle-aged man with the uniform of our district's Security Division came up to us. He knelt awkwardly in his stiff black trousers, slipped a small recording device out of his pocket and turned it on. "Mr. Manjali, I've got some questions for you," he said.

Chapter Twenty-Seven: Preen

Kiva kept smiling at me through his oxygen mask and reaching for my hand, though he couldn't hardly sit up straight. His skin was pimpled with the cold. The scrapes he'd got falling through the floor stood out harsh and red against the pale skin on his chest and back.

They gave him pills to swallow before they set the broken bone. The ED workers did it quick as they could, but it was awful to hear Kiva cry out when they pulled on his arm—made me cry, too.

After they'd wrapped the arm and put it in a sling, one of the men handed me another red and gray striped blanket, just like the one that covered Sanjit.

I wrapped it around Kiva's shoulders. We both trembled, him with cold, me with relief and joy. I hadn't been able to save Rama—maybe because he was set on not being saved—but with Kiva, God gave me another chance.

The men from the Rais's District Security Office took pictures of everything, the damage to the barn, the burned-out shell of the Sinds' house, Kiva and me sitting together on the ground. They took the blanket off Sanjit's body and took pictures of him and the gun he'd used to put an end to himself.

Kiva told the story of the morning into the recorder the officer with the moustache held out for him. He spoke in a hoarse whisper, pausing now and again to gulp more water from his bottle. He told the officer just about everything he knew about Sanjit and Rais Padmi and Rama and the things that had happened in Dor, but he left my name out of it.

When the officer left us, I laid my hand on Kiva's shoulder. "Erkan came."

"To the farm?"

"Yes." I waited for anger to flash into his eyes, but it didn't.

"Did he know anything about—"

I nodded. "Rama has a grave."

He laid his hand over mine. "That's good. Very good."

"And you'll never have to see Erkan again, because he's going to Canada."

"Canada. That's something," he said hoarsely.

I nodded. Neither of us knew anyone who'd traveled that far.

"You know, I was dead—pretty near, anyway—but here I am," Kiva went on. "God gave me my life back. So..." he rubbed hair out of his face with his good arm. "I don't really know how to say it except that I was a fool to be jealous of Erkan. Or to mistrust you."

"Can't blame you." I rubbed his shoulder through the coarse blanket.

"No. I was a fool." He cleared his throat and took another drink of water. "I think you get a clearer view of what's important in life after you almost die."

I wiped a smear of ash off his forehead with my sleeve. "Erkan told me he'd already warned Sanjit. But neither of us had any idea he'd do this when he found out."

We both looked around at the burned buildings, the smoke hanging in the air, the men rolling their big hoses back up onto the truck. "Or that you'd be caught up in it."

"None of this was your fault," he whispered before I could speak again. "I did the right thing, you did the right thing and Sanjit—he did what he wanted to do."

I tried not to look over at the trucks. "That's not what he wanted."

"Well, that's where the things he did want got him. But I think I underestimated him when I said he had no shame."

He eased his sling and bandaged arm aside with his other hand. "I wish—no, let's not talk about Sanjit. Let's talk about you. I didn't think nobody could hear me under the floor with all the noise they were making, but you—"

"Oh, I heard you. I'd hear you anywhere. No matter how quiet, no matter how far."

"Sharp ears." He brushed my earlobe with his thumb and set the hoop earring swinging.

"Saw your shirt, too, and I figured—"

"I thought I was going to die down there, fire or no fire," Kiva said. His eyes clouded over, chilly gray.

"You know what?"

"What?"

I pushed the damp locks out of his face. "The Emergency Department fellows helped, and Sanjit's horse helped—"

"Sanjit's horse?"

My smile let out a little of the glow inside. "Long story. They all helped, but God let me be the one. I found you. I saved you."

He nodded. "That's right. Preen, my guardian angel." He slipped the oxygen mask off his face, leaned forward, and kissed my lips. "I think God gave you the job so you'd understand you're forgiven."

***

Kiva didn't want to go to the hospital, but I made him go. We rode there together in the ambulance. At the hospital, they put an IV line in his arm and gave him a plaster cast.

He said he was feeling fine and we should just go home, but I told him he couldn't drive, and I couldn't drive, so we'd have to wait.

In the end, Arjun took us home. He also got Kiva's truck from the Sind farm. The truck wasn't burned at all.

***

The next day was Sunday. Sunday morning, I wore the green velour jacket Kiva had bought for me, and his grandmother's silver nose ring. It hung, heavy and expensive-looking, against my upper lip like a family heirloom should. For the first time since I took up with Rama, the size and extravagance of it made me proud instead of shamed. For the first time since I couldn't remember when, my heart held nothing but light.

Kiva sat in my family's pew, his right arm in a sling. I sat on his left, as close to him as I could get. We twined our fingers together under my bundled-up coat so nobody could say they saw us holding hands in church.

Sunday afternoon, Mother began sewing my wedding dress.

The End

Don't miss out!

Visit the website below and you can sign up to receive emails whenever E.B. Roshan publishes a new book. There's no charge and no obligation.

https://books2read.com/r/B-A-IESK-ZBDAC

BOOKS 2 READ

Connecting independent readers to independent writers.

Also by E.B. Roshan

Shards of Sevia
Wrong Place, Right Time
Final Chance
Love Costs
For Better and Worse
Judgment Call

Watch for more at https://shardsofsevia.wordpress.com.

About the Author

E.B. Roshan has enjoyed a nomadic lifestyle for several years, living in the Middle East, Asia and various places in the U.S. Now she is temporarily settled near Philadelphia with her husband and children. When she's not cooking, cleaning, or correcting math homework, she's writing the latest instalment in Shards of Sevia, her ongoing romantic suspense series set in the war-torn (and fortunately fictional) nation of Sevia. To learn more about E.B. Roshan and the Shards of Sevia series, visit: https://shardsofsevia.wordpress.com

Read more at https://shardsofsevia.wordpress.com.

www.ingramcontent.com/pod-product-compliance
Lightning Source LLC
Chambersburg PA
CBHW020958160726
47994CB00006B/2286